SHOLOM ALEICHEM, one of the most famous Yiddish writers,
was born in 1859 and died in New York in 1916. He is perhaps
best known for the "Tevye" stories, which were the basis for
the Broadway musical *Fiddler on the Roof.* His works include
Marienbad and several collections of short stories: *Holiday
Tales, Some Laughter, Some Tears, Old Country Tales,* and
Stories for Jewish Children.

ALIZA SHEVRIN is one of America's premier translators. Her
numerous translations from the Yiddish include some of the
novels and stories of Isaac Bashevis Singer and I. L. Peretz.
She translated the award-winning *Holiday Tales* and, most
recently, *Marienbad,* both by Sholom Aleichem.

In the Storm

BY SHOLOM ALEICHEM

translated by Aliza Shevrin

A PLUME BOOK

NEW AMERICAN LIBRARY

NEW YORK AND SCARBOROUGH, ONTARIO

NAL BOOKS ARE AVAILABLE AT QUANTITY DISCOUNTS WHEN USED TO
PROMOTE PRODUCTS OR SERVICES. FOR INFORMATION PLEASE WRITE
TO PREMIUM MARKETING DIVISION, NEW AMERICAN LIBRARY,
1633 BROADWAY, NEW YORK, NEW YORK 10019.

The author gratefully acknowledges permission from Howard Shevrin to print
his English translation of those parts of the Yiddish poem "In the City of Slaughter,"
by Chaim Nachman Bialik, which appear in this book.

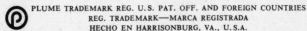 PLUME TRADEMARK REG. U.S. PAT. OFF. AND FOREIGN COUNTRIES
REG. TRADEMARK—MARCA REGISTRADA
HECHO EN HARRISONBURG, VA., U.S.A.

SIGNET, SIGNET CLASSIC, MENTOR, PLUME, MERIDIAN and
NAL BOOKS are published *in the United States* by New American Library,
1633 Broadway, New York, New York 10019,
in Canada by The New American Library of Canada Limited,
81 Mack Avenue, Scarborough, Ontario M1L 1M8

Library of Congress Cataloging-in-Publication Data

Sholom Aleichem, 1859–1916.
  In the storm.

  Translation of: In shturm.
  I. Title.
PJ5129.R2I5313   1985   839'.0933   85-11072
ISBN 0-452-25760-3

First Plume Printing, September, 1985

1 2 3 4 5 6 7 8 9

PRINTED IN THE UNITED STATES OF AMERICA

For

myne tyere kinder,

Dan and his wife Carol,
Amy, David and Matt

and for

di zisse einiklech,

Ilene and Julie

mit libbe

Translator's Introduction

"Very few writers have surpassed Sholom Aleichem in re-creating that atmosphere of radiant hope and idealism which preceded the granting of the 1905 Constitution, or the ghastly psychological let-down which followed the treacherous retraction," Maurice Samuels has noted in *The World of Sholom Aleichem* in praise of *In the Storm*. Set in Russia at the turn of the century, *In the Storm* is a novel of social, political and personal upheaval, a novel in which the Jewish and gentile protagonists play varying roles in the turbulent events leading up to the abortive October Revolution. It was written first as a serial and published in 1907 in the periodicals *Varheit* (Truth) and *Unzer Lebn* (Our Life), under the title *Der Mabl* (The Deluge). Sholom Aleichem often reworked his published material, and *Der Mabl* later appeared in book form as *In Shturm*.

By 1905 Sholom Aleichem had achieved considerable success and could now make his living entirely from his writing and from giving public readings. Many Yiddish periodicals and newspapers had made their appearance, and he was in his element. As his daughter, Marie Waife-Goldberg, pointed out in her biography, *My Father, Sholom Aleichem,* some of his best stories (including several of the Tevye stories) were written and published in the early 1900s.

These were also the years when world events were disrupting the lives of every Jew in Russia. The czarist regime had decided to cease compromising with the masses and attempted to divert their attention from worsening economic conditions, widespread strikes and repression by turning their frustration against the Jews. One consequence was the bloody Kishinev pogrom that took place on Easter Sunday 1903.

Pogroms had become a systematic, integral part of czarist policy. Russian Jews had been haunted by the specter of pogroms since the gruesome massacres in Odessa in 1820, 1859, 1871, and more frequently still in the 1880s. Still, Russian Jewry was shocked by the sheer brutality of the Kishinev pogrom as well as by the almost complete indifference on the part of the non-Jewish populace, including the liberal Social Democrats. It was clear that the police had followed the Czar's orders in organizing the pogrom and then failing to stop it. Despite these efforts to vent popular frustration through pogroms, a surge of agitation against the autocracy of Nicholas II developed, and, fueled by Russia's humiliating defeat at the hands of the Japanese, this discontent reached its boiling point on Bloody Sunday, January 9, 1905. Several hundred thousand Russians, carrying icons and chanting prayers, led by the priest Father Gapon, petitioned the Czar at his Winter Palace in St. Petersburg for moderate reforms. The crowd was fired upon and many were slain.

In the novel Sholom Aleichem describes these events in historically accurate detail. After the shock of Bloody Sunday, in March 1905, the Czar promised to convoke a duma, a consultative assembly, but that was perceived as insufficient and the masses were inflamed all the more. There followed assassinations, revolutionary and subversive acts, strikes, and mutinies. In October the Czar yielded and issued a manifesto granting the full demands of the people—a constitutional government that would grant all basic liberties and legislative powers to the people. Sholom Aleichem himself shared in the many celebrations and congratulations of this new era of elation and optimism. It was to be short-lived. The Czar retracted the constitution, which released a torrent of reaction and terror, arrests and suppression, and an outbreak of officially inspired pogroms far exceeding in terror the one in Kishinev. The Black Hundreds, bands of hoodlums whose slogan was "Kill the Jews and Save Russia," were joined by local thugs and anti-Semites. Savage pogroms occurred in at least six hundred and sixty Jewish communities in Russia.

The October pogrom in Kiev abruptly changed the life of Sholom Aleichem and his large family. His daughter's account of the family's experience of this pogrom is worth quoting: "It was suggested we move to a hotel until the danger was over, which we did. . . . We were awakened by a terrifying noise. . . . Loud shouts and shrill cries. We ran from our beds to the window on the street and looked down at a scene of brutality and murder—a gang of hoodlums beating a poor young Jew with heavy sticks; blood was running over the face of the young man, who was vainly shrieking for aid. A policeman stood nearby, casually looking on. Our mother pulled the shade and ordered us never to go near the windows. . . . The Kiev pogroms lasted

9

three days, three terrible days and nights during which we were unable to sleep or eat, walking in silence and fear. The rage of hate and evil finally subsided and it was safe to return to our apartment. . . . Life returned to normality, although it was never to be the same again."

An unprecedented surge of emigration poured from Russia—over a hundred thousand people a year were leaving, mainly Jews, mostly to America. In 1906 Sholom Aleichem began a period of wandering that was to continue the rest of his life. It was in Switzerland that he started to publish the present novel in installments.

He used the events leading up to and including the granting and retraction of the constitution and the 1905 pogroms as the historical background of this novel. His main characters belong to two generations of three families of different philosophies, religious commitments, and socioeconomic status, all living in one apartment house in Kiev. Their heterogeneity provides him with the opportunity to explore various degrees of assimilation and rebellion played out on the small scale of family life but held up against the vast canvas of Russian political life. Not only were parents and children opposed to one another as they struggled with ideas of social equality for all classes as well as for the sexes, but the young people themselves were also in opposition to one another ideologically. The revolutionary socialists were hardly identified with the plight of the Jews, nor were they eager to promote a Jewish state or language; their identity was with the Russian people as a whole, their enemy the czarist regime. A few young idealists, such as Sasha, the son of the assimilated pharmacist, stood up for Jewish freedom and regeneration, which they believed had to be a priority for Jews.

In the novel Sholom Aleichem makes special use of the Jewish paschal holiday of Pesach, or Passover—the springtime commemoration of the exodus from Egypt, the passing over from slavery to hard-won freedom and nationhood. Skillfully he brings together the sprouting of new hope in Jew and gentile alike for an enlightened Russia and the ritual family celebration around the festive Pesach seder table. In so doing, Sholom Aleichem draws on the special genius of the Jewish people for transforming what is given in nature into historically significant acts binding God and man together. It is not enough to celebrate the arrival of spring—that would simply be pagan; the holiday must also signify a historical event, the exodus, and remind God of his promise of freedom and man of his responsibility to ensure or obtain it.

Pesach is an especially joyous holiday, intimate and familial in spirit, but it is also a reminder of past deliverance and the hope of future deliverance. The permissive feasting and drinking are moderated by a religious service, so that, for example, only a certain number of goblets of wine are to be drunk, and those at specific times, each having a special significance. The Jewish spirit tends to harness both nature and natural impulses to social and moral purposes. When practiced to excess, this attitude has led to empty formalism and an alienation from the natural, so that the zealously pious Jew may always have felt a vague uneasiness in the midst of nature's rich profusion and temptations. It is no accident that the two gardens mentioned in the novel both belong to gentiles, and one of them is envied by the hardworking Jewish merchant, who wonders if it isn't Esau, with his wild country ways, rather than Jacob, who got the better deal.

In addition to his artistic use of Passover, Sholom Aleichem has introduced another significant Jewish institution into the novel—the writings of the great

Hebrew and Yiddish poet Chaim Nachman Bialik (1873–1934). Bialik's searing and elegiac poems exercised a profound influence on modern Jewish culture, as well as on his contemporaries, including Sholom Aleichem. After the Kishinev pogrom Bialik visited that city on behalf of the Odessa Jewish Historical Commission to interview survivors and to prepare a report on that atrocity. The year following, 1904, he wrote a Yiddish poem, "In the City of Slaughter," portions of which are quoted in the novel (translated by my husband, Howard Shevrin). The poem describes the brutal massacre to which the Jews of Kishinev meekly submitted and serves in the novel to foreshadow its repetition within a short time. Sholom Aleichem assigns to a poor wood hauler, the bereaved father of the heroine, the role of the prophet who predicts the coming of the deluge. Tragically, the events of World War II were to prove all those prophecies to be correct. Kishinev was repeated endlessly, to the grief and sorrow of the modern world.

Sholom Aleichem describes his meeting with Bialik in a charming sketch, "My Acquaintance with Bialik," written in 1916, the year of his death, and published in a collection, *Yiddishe Shreiber* (Yiddish Writers). Because Sholom Aleichem lived in Kiev and Bialik in Odessa, the two had never met, although they knew of each other, until both were delegates to the 1907 Zionist Congress held at The Hague and were attending a conference of Hebraists. They became constant companions, spending many hours together, talking as if they had known each other for years. Bialik visited Sholom Aleichem in Geneva, and they corresponded until Sholom Aleichem's death.

The immense popularity of *Fiddler on the Roof* has left the impression that Sholom Aleichem was primarily a writer about poverty-stricken shtetl life, somewhat provincial, depicting his people's lifelong struggle for dignity and survival. Although this is true, it is not the whole truth. Sholom Aleichem loved and was loved by those he referred to as *"die kleine menshelech"* (the little people), and was indeed their chronicler and spokesman in Yiddish literature; he was, in addition—especially in his later, more affluent years—a sophisticated, worldly, cultured man who numbered among his circle many of the leading literary, political, and artistic figures of the day. He traveled widely, entertained elegantly at home with the help of servants, and was well read in the works of his great literary contemporaries. His wife was a practicing dentist, his children well educated.

Sholom Aleichem's full participation in modern European culture, particularly his approach to women, is reflected in the novel, in which female figures play central roles. Both heroines, Tamara and Masha, are the favorites, if not the obsessions of their fathers, almost to the exclusion of everyone and everything else. Masha is the most effective member of her revolutionary circle and is the pivotal character in the book. Both women seem to be sources of confusion to their old-fashioned fathers, who are simply baffled by their daughters' independent actions, challenges, and confrontations. The fathers' roles as matchmakers and decision-makers are no longer accepted as in past generations. Tamara will become a doctor and will not hear of her father's objections; she encourages her mother to follow her in rebellion. And all this in 1905!

The translator's task is not very different from that of a musician or actor. One is presented with a manuscript (score or script) that, it is assumed, will be rendered into another art form (the performance itself) as loyally and exactly as its author intended. While the interpreter or performer adheres as closely as possible to the original, there is still a great deal of latitude. The translator often encounters obvious flaws, inconsistencies, or so-called untranslatable words, phrases, or idioms that are time- or culture-bound or have no real equivalents in contemporary language. An example: Early in the novel one of the characters enters a room and is asked by another, "Why are you so *B'rifidim'dik?*" It is impossible to guess from the context what that might mean, and the word does not exist in any form in Yiddish or Hebrew dictionaries. However, in a chance conversation with a good friend, Herbert Paper, of Hebrew Union College, the mystery was solved. Riphidim is the place in Exodus where the Israelites rebelled against Moses because they had run out of water. So Sholom Aleichem, using a Hebrew prefix, a Biblical place-name, and a Slavic or Germanic (depending on one's linguistic theory) suffix, coined a word. I came up with "rebellious," which is close but in no way captures the speaker's Biblical allusion, his fastidious use of Hebrew, or his need to impress others with his knowledge.

Because of the inherent limitations of the forms themselves it is inevitable that some nuances will be lost in translation. The translator must take certain liberties, while avoiding the temptation to edit, "improve," or simplify the original. In this lies the creative challenge of translation, its pleasure, and, at the same time, its greatest frustration. Many hours were spent tracking down obscure words, some details of which I would like to share with the reader.

Toward the end of the book one character tells another she wishes he would visit her garden so she could give him some of her delicious *shpankes,* which from the context clearly refers to a fruit. But what fruit? It was nowhere to be found. Again, a lucky meeting. My dormitory neighbor at the 1983 Yiddish Conference at Somerville College, Oxford, was Dr. Mordkhe Schaechter, of Columbia University, a specialist in Yiddish botanical terms. *Shpankes,* he told me, are Yellow Spanish cherries.

But not every quest ended in success. One of the characters, in a state of madness, prophesies doom, chanting the refrain, "Egeden, magaden, magdaden . . ." I ran into a dead end; all efforts to identify those words were fruitless. Is it simply a string of nonsense syllables made up by a deranged man or do those words mean something in a language unknown to me or any of my consultants? And then there was the problem of Yudel Katanti, the character whose speech to his Yiddish- and Russian-speaking fellow characters is strewn with Biblical Hebrew malapropisms. Even translated, these expressions would simply confuse readers unfamiliar with Biblical Hebrew, and I have taken the liberty of deleting some of them.

I have been fortunate in having the help of several native Russians in the Ann Arbor Yiddish Club, in particular Basya Genkina and Anya Finkel, who were acquainted with many of the colloquial terms used in the novel. Members of the University of Michigan Comparative Literature Translation Seminar patiently heard several chapters in preparation. Robert Danly, organizer of this seminar and himself a distinguished translator of Japanese literature, was of enormous help. Also, I wish to thank Bel Kaufman, Professors Arthur Mendel, Zvi Gitelman, Maurice Friedberg, Serge Shishkoff, Anita Norich, my wonderful typist Dorothy Foster, and, most especially, my beloved parents, Rabbi Eliezer and Rivka Goldberger, my "living dictionaries." Again, as in other projects, my husband was a constant source of editorial help, offering an alternative word when I was stuck, working closely with me, and, of course, translating the Bialik poem.

I wish to express my special gratitude to the Rockefeller Foundation for the opportunity to spend a month as scholar-in-residence at its Study and Conference Center in the glorious Villa Serbelloni in Bellagio on Lake Como, Italy, where I was able to translate half of this volume. I cannot reread the words I worked on there without picturing in my mind's eye the magnificent panorama of crystal-clear lake and snow-capped mountains I saw every day from my studio.

Aliza Shevrin
Ann Arbor, Michigan
September 1983

PART ONE

1

Pesach, Pesach, and Pesach

Three different Pesachs were being prepared at No. 13 Vasilchikover Street.

In fact, it was one and the same Passover—the same matzos, the same bitter herbs, the same Haggadah. The difference was in the way the holiday was prepared, observed, and celebrated, because the people living at No. 13 Vasilchikover Street were quite different people, with different personalities and different points of view.

At No. 13 Vasilchikover Street lived three men. And each of the three was positive that only his God was the true God, that only his understanding was the correct understanding, and that only for his sake had this little world been created.

You might suppose that these three were people from different faiths, from different backgrounds, and from different countries?

God forbid! All three believed in the same God, all

three shared the same background, and all three came from the same part of the country.

These three Russian Jews the author of this novel now has the honor of introducing to his readers: Itzikl Shostepol, Solomon Safranovitch, and Nehemiah the shoemaker.

Itzikl! The name alone tells you that this must be a Jew steeped in tradition, a Jew who might deal in timber, in subcontracting, in grain; or he might be the kind of man who owned a fine shop, a manufacturing business, or a glass factory; or he might be a supplier for the prisons and the army barracks, splitting the profits with the warden or the commissary officer fifty-fifty, pampering the inmates and the troops with gruel and gristle. But if he were none of these, Itzikl might be a money-lender, not for exorbitant interest, heaven forbid, or one who would dun his clients weekly, but a businesslike banker, with checks and bank drafts, who wouldn't go after large profits but would encourage trust, lend out mortgage money, select reliable backers and solid investments.

In any case, Itzikl was regarded in the community as one of the finest, most dependable, and respected citizens. He was everywhere, and everywhere you heard "Itzikl Shostepol! Itzikl Shostepol!" Was a celebration going on, a gathering, a town meeting? There was Itzikl Shostepol. Was there, God forbid, a crisis, a funeral, a tragedy, a fire, an epidemic, a pogrom? There was Itzikl Shostepol. Were they raising funds? There was Itzikl Shostepol. Was there a complaint to be made? There was Itzikl Shostepol. The truth could not be escaped— Itzikl Shostepol could complain very ably. But he wasn't as generous with his money as he was with his politicking and complaining.

Should you ever visit my town or should you ever be

on a train and meet an absentminded character with smooth, rosy cheeks, with very shiny black (now graying) hair, with a curly little beard that he constantly braids and twists and tugs at, with large fine dark Jewish eyes (a woman possessing them would drive men mad), with a slightly bent, typically Jewish nose, with a small hat that is always pushed back on one side of his head, with rolled-up sleeves, and with an umbrella under his arm both summer and winter—should you meet such a person, go right up to him on my account, don't be afraid, and say to him, "Sholom aleichem, Reb Itzikl!"

He will gaze at you with his fine dark Jewish eyes, smile politely, stretch out a fine white soft hand, and reply, "Aleichem sholom to you. How are you?"

He won't ask you who you are or what your name is, because if you have honored him with a "Sholom aleichem," you probably already know him. And who doesn't know him? From the poorest beggar to the wealthiest and most aristocratic rich man, from the worst traif'nik to the strictest frum'nik—everyone knows Itzikl Shostepol, and Itzikl Shostepol knows everyone, gets along with everyone, is everyone's friend, and is on intimate terms with the whole world.

And the whole world loves such people. The whole world loves a person who caters to others and lets himself be catered to, the whole world loves a person who smiles at others and who invites smiles in return, who deceives others and allows others to deceive him, who steps on others and lets himself be stepped on. The whole world is of the opinion that principles, ideals, and the like are fine on paper, but in real life they are nonsense—adolescent pipe dreams.

Come with me, reader, give me your hand, let us proceed—we have a long, long way to go!

The second person who lived at No. 13 Vasilchikover

Street was Solomon Safranovitch the pharmacist, of that type of pharmacist who eats sausage dipped in sour cream, goes unwashed and without a hat on Yom Kippur, and despises Jews in the extreme, and only because no other people has as many redheads as the Jewish people. One can almost agree with him. How many gentiles have you seen with red hair? He himself was a redhead, his father was a redhead; his sister, however, was a blonde. He had a son—Sasha was his name (we will soon get acquainted with him)—and he too was a redhead.

Picture, if you can, Solomon dyeing his hair, shaving his beard, not allowing so much as a single red hair to show in his head or beard. But what does one do about one's eyebrows? What Solomon Safranovitch wouldn't have given to have been born with black hair!

But all this took place a long time ago. Today our Safranovitch is no longer a redhead. He is entirely white-haired. His hair turned prematurely white because of great worries over his child.

One child, the one and only Sasha—and so many worries! And why so many worries, you might wonder. Was he a problem child? Uninterested in school? A poor student? A stupid boy? Not at all, quite the opposite. Sasha was a fine boy, with a good head on his shoulders, eager to learn. At the age of ten he was ready to enter not only the first but the third class of Gymnasium. But the problem was that they wouldn't accept him because of the quotas. I don't have to go into detail to explain what I mean by the quotas. It is well known that in our blessed Russia, Jews are dealt with on the basis of quotas. In the Gymnasia and universities they accept fewer and fewer Jewish students, but should a military draft take place, then Jews are accepted without a quota, so that their feelings won't be hurt.

Ach, how poor Solomon Safranovitch suffered, how he grieved, how he aggravated himself! It was his only son, his Sasha, they wouldn't accept in Gymnasium. To begin with, Safranovitch wasn't like any of the other Jews—he knew the director of the Gymnasium, he knew the teachers well, even played cards with them. He once had a chat about his son with one of the teachers, Romanenko was his name, and was rudely rebuffed in a typically gentile manner.

"What is it that you want? Where are you pushing your son? What business do you Jews have in our schools, Gymnasia, universities? There, in your own country, in Palestine, you can educate your children. Here you should teach them lending and spending, wheeling and dealing!"

Boiling with rage, our pharmacist left the teacher, not knowing where to hide those gray eyes with the red eyebrows behind the blue-tinted spectacles. Most painful were the words "your own country, Palestine." He, Solomon Safranovitch, had as much to do with Palestine as Romanenko had to do with fairness. On the contrary, in town it was well known that Safranovitch the pharmacist was a fanatic anti-Zionist on principle who hated the newly emerging Jewish partisans calling themselves nationalists, hated them even more than Itzikl Shostepol hated the socialist scoundrels who wanted to divide among the rest of the world his bit of poverty.

How remarkable it is the way God chooses to run the world! As luck would have it, to this pharmacist, to this old-time traif'nik and latter-day anti-Zionist, was born a son, Sasha, who became an ardent, dedicated nationalist. And to the bourgeois Itzikl Shostepol, who was more frightened of a socialist than of a Russian policeman, was born a daughter, Tema, or Tamara, a fanatic, committed socialist!

The third person who lived at No. 13 was Nehemiah the shoemaker. Nehemiah the shoemaker was a shlimazel. So he was called by his wife, Zissel, a short dark-haired woman with small black piercing eyes and no front teeth. Looking at this emaciated little woman and at her two sons, Chaim and Benny, two tall, healthy, husky giants, one would find it impossible to believe that this was the mother and these were her children. Nor did the father, Nehemiah, bear any resemblance to his sons. Nehemiah was a squarely built Jew, a hairy, barrel-chested, big-boned, broad-backed man with a wide, bony face and a flat nose, who loved two things—a little brandy and a lot of talk. He never shut up for a moment. But if he drank so much as a drop of brandy, he would become silent and morose. Just the opposite of his friend Yudel.

Although he was a tailor by trade, Yudel's main pre-occupations were politics—the problems of the day and city hall shenanigans. Colloquially he would be called a busybody—he busied himself talking about politics because most of the time he didn't have a stitch of work, and as a result he was poor and had in him endless yardage of talk. People called him Katanti—the Hebrew word for "small one"—because he always used Hebrew in his speech. After every two or three words of Yiddish he had to throw in a Hebrew word, no matter whether it was suitable or not, so long as it was Hebrew. There are many such people who love to ornament and mix their own language with foreign words. I knew a man from a small town, an adherent of the Haskalah, an intellectual, who peppered his speech with foreign words all the time and was therefore nicknamed "Yisroelik Civilizatzia." And in a small town, when you are given a nickname it is custom-made—as Yudel Katanti would say, *"agil v'asmach"*—joy and happiness—

incorrectly translating it into his tailor's language as "perfectly cut to measure."

An uncanny and touching friendship existed between these two strangely different souls, Yudel Katanti and Nehemiah the shoemaker. Not a day passed that Yudel did not drop in at Nehemiah the shoemaker's for a "short visit," and a "short visit" meant a bit of a chat, and a bit of a chat meant a little gossiping about the neighbors, the town, the whole world. Even before Yudel had crossed the threshold you could hear a cough and "A curse upon their fathers, these common Jews, our own people, may a disaster befall them, a plague, a conflagration, a pestilence unto the last generation." And Nehemiah would respond in a singsong, "So be it, amen! What's the matter, Yudel, why are you so, so . . . ?"

"So what? Rebellious?" Yudel Katanti filled in. "A curse unto their fathers' fathers unto Adam himself for the way they have blighted our years and our days with their demonstrations and their way of life and their good deeds and their having pity on poor people who don't have so much as a crumb with which to celebrate Pesach."

"Again?" broke in the shoemaker's wife, Zissel. "Two shlimazels put their heads together and are worrying about poor people not having enough for Pesach. So, do *you* have everything ready for Pesach? Go on home! God willing, come back on yomtov when there is no housework to be done. *Then* you can talk to your heart's content."

And Zissel the shoemaker's wife sent the tailor off and went back to her housecleaning—sweeping, polishing, washing, scouring. Whether there was enough for Pesach or not, it had to be kosher for the holidays, and the house had to be clean and tidy. That was a must for both rich and poor. Even the most wretched of the wretched had to have the same kosher, clean and tidy Pesach. For all Jews alike, for all Jews at the same time: the same matzos, the same *arba koses*—four goblets of wine—four: no more, no fewer. In this sameness there dwelt a deep satisfaction, a boon for the poor common man, who in these ways need not feel inferior to the rich man.

"Tell me, does Itzikl Shostepol have different matzos from ours?" demanded Nehemiah the shoemaker, and received from his skeptical wife, Zissel, the usual compliment.

"Some example! Itzikl Shostepol already has *his* matzos in the pantry, while our pantry is empty."

"We'll have matzos too, Zissel, don't worry. Every Jew will have matzos for Pesach. No one will eat chometz, God forbid."

"Shlimazel! Nu, and eggs? And schmaltz? And chicken? Have you forgotten?"

"So, hasn't Itzikl had the same eggs and shmaltz and chicken the rest of the year?" The shoemaker attempted to triumph over his wife's skepticism and offered her yet another argument. "Isn't it true that we will all sit down at the same time to the same seder, we will all read from the same Haggadah, we will all tell of the same miracles from the same Egypt, and we will all drink the same four goblets of wine? Or perhaps you think we will drink three glasses, while Itzikl Shostepol drinks five glasses?"

"Do you want to know what I think? I think he's already got his wine in his cellar, while you still have yours only in your head."

"What do I care whether I have it in my head or not, silly? What's so terrible if even now I have in mind the thought of a little schnapps, of some good wine, a really

26

good Bessarabian glass of wine—delicious, strong, tangy?"

"What do you say to this shlimazel?" These words were spoken to the children, Chaim and Benny, who were seated at the workbench, hammers in hand, nailing tacks into soles.

"What can we say?" the older, Chaim, replied for both of them. "We can only say that he who doesn't have enough to eat has every right to think about eating, and not only to think about it but to think about how everyone should have enough to eat."

"That was already foretold by Moshe Rabeynu," said Nehemiah the shoemaker, borrowing from some of Yudel the tailor's knowledge of the Torah.

"Moshe Rabeynu was a fine person," contributed the younger son, Benny. "He promised us all the same matzos for Pesach, the same Haggadah, and the same four goblets of wine. Why didn't he at the same time see to it that we were *all* provided with these things? But for now we know that Itzikl Shostepol has his matzos and four goblets of wine, while we have no more than the Haggadah."

"To us he assigned the Haggadah in order for us to have something to read while they sit and enjoy kugel and chremsel," said Chaim.

"May they choke on it, God in heaven!" Zissel took the opportunity to toss in a curse.

"Why do they deserve to be cursed?" asked Nehemiah. "Why are they guilty, my dear, for what we don't have for Pesach?"

"Because *they* have and *we* don't—*that's* why they're guilty!" Zissel reasoned, assuming the manner of a rabbi explaining something to a slow student. "If you weren't such a shlimazel, you yourself would understand that if *they* had less *we* would have more, and then it would all be even."

"Mama is a Marxist!" Chaim exclaimed to Benny, and Benny answered, "We ought to take her along to one of our discussions. Mama, would you like to come to one of our discussions?"

"I'd sooner go to hell! You're forgetting it's erev Pesach and I've only finished the front rooms. If only that shlimazel there would remind himself that except for potatoes we have nothing—not a scrap of shmaltz, no eggs, not a chicken."

Suddenly the sound of "cluck-cluck, cluck-cluck!" was heard from the rooster that all this time was quietly sitting hidden under the stove pecking at crumbs until, hearing those words from the shoemaker's wife, it also seemed to take offense, as if saying, "Cluck-cluck, am I not a chicken too?"

"Aha! Do you see?" Nehemiah the shoemaker said to his wife. "You were just complaining you had no chicken for Pesach—so what's this?"

"You call that a chicken?" Zissel replied. "Do you know what you'll get from that kind of chicken? Three pounds of bones, a half pound of shoe leather, meat like rubber from galoshes, and not so much as an ounce of fat to grease the frying pan in case one of the children gets an urge to have a latke or some fried matzos. You should see the two turkeys strutting around Itzikl Shostepol's place, a male and a female. May a miracle occur, God in heaven, may they both become unkosher at the same time. Oh, that would be my greatest pleasure, my greatest reward!"

"So what would you gain by it?" asked her husband.

"It would serve them right! How come *he* deserves to get so much? Why does *his* daughter, who was raised in the same house, in the same courtyard as *ours,* study in classes and play the piano, while our daughter has to sit bent over a machine, barely earning enough for a cheap dress?"

"Whom can you blame for that?" countered Nehemiah, looking at her through his strange spectacles, which had but one lens.

"Not you, shlimazel. I blame God."

"Don't blame God, blame people," put in the elder son, Chaim. "God Himself created the world equally for everyone, but people divided it unequally."

"One gets everything, the other nothing," the younger, Benny, continued.

Zissel reflected a moment, laid aside her work, dried her hands on her apron, and asked her children in all seriousness, "So what's to be done?"

"What's to be done?" Chaim repeated slowly. "Expropriation!"

"Ex— what?" asked Zissel.

"Expropriation," repeated Benny.

Zissel tried to pronounce the word but couldn't. She spat in disgust, went back to her sweeping, and both sons burst out laughing.

The shoemaker's wife's outrage was somewhat justified. There were more than a pair of turkeys strutting around Itzikl Shostepol's yard, splitting one's ears with their gobbling and befouling the way wherever one stepped.

One had to see for oneself the chicken coop full to bursting with roosting hens, pecking at their feed and accumulating shmaltz for their mistress, Itzikl Shostepol's wife, Shivka, the rich woman. And if one weren't too lazy to look into her pantry, one would see pots of Pesach shmaltz alongside jars of Pesach preserves, and in the cellar one would see kegs of pickles and marinated apples—nothing but the best! And Pesach brandy and cognac, real Carmel cognac from Israel, which was bought over a year ago. How happy they must be, how clear their heads must be, how free of worry their minds must be to remember to save cognac from one year to the next. Yet if one spoke to Itzikl Shostepol, he wouldn't stop moaning and groaning about the problems of the Jews, and he would tell you how hard life was.

Also Shivka, his wife, kept bewailing and bemoaning the Jewish plight. How can you tolerate such poverty? she would say. Where does one get the strength to witness the squalor in this city? You have to have the heart of a Tartar, she would say, to be able to walk down the street before Pesach. How the poor folk tug at your skirts! Only a criminal, she would say, could walk down the Shul Street and listen to all the weeping and wailing of the poor people begging for matzos for Pesach. That's why, she would say, I don't go out of the house—so I won't have to see the suffering and the anguish of the Jewish people. As much as I am able, she said, I give. I sent over a ruble and a half to be distributed and I donated a pair of shoes to the Clothing Society. I gave the tailor a few rubles as an advance toward some sewing and I hand out alms every day, not to mention the Pesach Charity. My husband works day and night to contribute to the Pesach Charity, may God help me, may my daughter come home safely and may I have, God willing, a kosher and happy Pesach.

Itzikl Shostepol's wife, Shivka, looked out the window on Vasilchikover Street, where the erev-Pesach slush was ankle-deep, where the poor people were slogging through the mud, sweating and straining to eke out a groschen or two for Pesach. Alongside them the poor horses toiled—emaciated, starved, perspiring, with sunken flanks and sagging nostrils. Only God could know which deserved more pity—those exhausted four-legged mute creatures who served their poverty-stricken masters so loyally or their hardly more fortunate two-legged masters who trudged behind them, whooping and bellowing, commanding and whipping, flogging and lashing their faded, scarred coats. The horses seemed to be saying, "Why are you whooping? Why are you bellowing? Why are you commanding? Why are you whipping? Why are you flogging? Why are you lashing our poor bodies? Foolish people! Don't you see that we want to work, we want to pull, but we can't, we can barely stumble about on our weakened legs!"

And Shivka, the rich woman, looked out her window and saw all of this, heard the shouting and the tumult outside, but her mind was elsewhere. Her thoughts were with her daughter, who was coming home for Pesach. A telegram had already arrived saying that she would be coming by express train that very evening.

With God's help, thought Shivka, the child will return home safely and put aside this nonsense—studying and an education. Better for her to remain at home. Here she can get married, either to Shimshon Bernstein's son or to Levi Halpern's son. Both are fine young men, handsome and wealthy, and both from good families. I myself would find it hard to decide which of the two was better.

"The Jew delivering the wood is here and wishes to see you," said one of the housemaids.

"What does that shlimazel want from me? I'll be right there." And Shivka Shostepol went out to see the Jew with the wood, Lippa by name. He was a small man, but his beard was like a broom, and she thought he looked a bit bewildered. What was he pestering her about? It appeared he had a daughter, who was in prison, and since her daughter, Tamara, once knew his daughter, he was asking if there were regards for him. This idiot, Lippa, made her nervous, and she lashed out at him as only a rich woman can lash out at a poor man.

"In the first place, who do you think you are, talking about our daughters as if they were friends? And in the second place, what does my daughter have to do with her when you yourself aren't ashamed to tell me she's in prison?"

"Why should I be ashamed?" answered the wood hauler, smoothing his broom beard with pride. "She isn't in prison, God forbid, for stealing. She is a political prisoner."

Before he spoke the words "political prisoner" he looked around on all sides, and once he had spoken the words, one realized that he was both proud and sorry to have said them.

"Get out of here and leave us alone with your nonsense. My daughter has nothing to do with these things, and we certainly don't."

"Nothing, you say? Hmm. Perhaps you are mistaken," so answered Lippa. But Shivka wasn't listening anymore; she had left him standing with his broom beard and had vanished into the kitchen, where she berated the servants for allowing every vagrant with muddy boots into the house. She resumed her seat at the window and waited for her daughter, who would soon be coming home.

At the same time another person was sitting at his window in that same No. 13 Vasilchikover Street, waiting for a very welcome guest. This was Solomon Safranovitch the pharmacist. He had also received a telegram from his son, Sasha, announcing that he was traveling by express train and would be arriving home that very evening.

Sasha was at the university, studying medicine. It had been almost a year since his father had seen him. There had been frequent, fine letters, and the pharmacist was very proud of his son. But recently strange new words had begun to appear in his son's letters, such words as "Jews," "the people," "nationalism," "debt," "history." How did these words come to Sasha? And what good were they to him? For his son's sake Solomon Safranovitch had made many sacrifices in order to see him complete Gymnasium and enter the university. The pharmacist had only one purpose in life—to see Sasha become a doctor. He asked for nothing more. Well, that was what he *said*. He really asked for much more—a fine office for Sasha's practice and a handsome horse and carriage with which to visit his patients. But for that, money was needed, and money could be obtained only through a good match with someone from a wealthy family who could afford a dowry of at least twenty-five thousand rubles! A thought struck him: Itzikl Shostepol's daughter—a fine girl . . . a brunette with fiery eyes . . . There was certainly money to be had and lots of it, but the question was whether that stingy swine, that Itzikl Shostepol, would want to part with twenty-five thousand. To the devil with him! If he doesn't want a match, we don't either. I need him like I need a hole in the head, that frum'nik, that hypocrite, that Jew with the umbrella!

Thus our pharmacist sat at his window, peering through his blue-tinted spectacles, thinking about his son, Sasha, and building castles in the air on his behalf. And his son, Sasha? Sasha was sitting in a second-class carriage with Itzikl Shostepol's daughter, Tamara, discussing the question of nationalism and cosmopolitan-

33

ism with her, all the while gazing at her intelligent dark gentle eyes that seemed to look right inside him, laughing at him and caressing him at the same time while drawing him to her with an irresistible power.

"What do you expect me to do?" Tamara said to him with a little laugh. "Do you expect me to give up the highest ideal in the world, to shut my ears and not hear the cries of a hundred million people who are crying for bread and freedom for the benefit of a handful of people who suffer no more and no less than all the others? Just because we are of the same religion and we share the same history and are called by the same name?"

"—and have the same eyes and are stamped with the same noses." Sasha finished the sentence for her.

"Now is not the time to look at such things," Tamara answered him.

"And yet people look hard at those very things," said Sasha. "Let me tell you what I have to put up with from my friends at the university because of the color of my hair."

"Ay-ay-ay!" Tamara interrupted him. "They've surely been teasing you about your red hair? First of all, it's the truth," she laughed, "and second of all, how can you compare that suffering with the suffering of the entire Russian people at the hands of the regime?"

"If the entire Russian people suffer, then our suffering is double—first as Russians and second as Jews."

"What do you think carries more weight, Monsieur Safranovitch, the suffering of a whole nation or the suffering of your own Jewish people?"

"It's not a matter of weighing and balancing, Fraulein Shostepol. It would be as if you were to ask me as a physician what would be worse, to cut off a finger or a toe? To that I would answer: bad as it is for one to lose a finger *or* a toe, it is twice as bad for one to lose a finger *and* a toe. And if you wish, Fraulein Shostepol, I'll tell you a secret. The sufferings of the Jewish people upset me far more than the sufferings of mankind. Do you know why? Because to these general sufferings are added humiliation and heartache. Why should we as Jews be persecuted by the persecuted and enslaved by the enslaved?"

Tamara Shostepol sat up straight and her lovely dark eyes ignited like two flames.

"Not true, Herr Safranovitch, not true! Do you hear what I am saying? I am saying that you and all your colleagues, the nationalists, have invented the lie that we are being persecuted by the Russian people. It's a lie— we are being persecuted by the bureaucracy, not by the people! You are either great liars or great fools!"

"If that's the case, then we have nothing more to say to each other"—and Sasha Safranovitch turned away from her and looked out the train window.

"Ha-ha-ha!" Tamara laughed and moved closer to him, looking directly into his eyes. "I didn't mean you, but your friends. I wasn't including you."

"Oh, thank you very much!" Sasha answered her and looked into her eyes against his will, wondering all the while about the mysterious power that lay behind those two dark windows that had so bewitched him, so enchanted and enslaved him that he was prepared to bear every kind of insult to keep before him those two large, beautiful, deep, dark, intelligent eyes.

2

Children and Parents, Parents and Children

If I were to characterize the romance of Sasha Safranovitch and Tamara Shostepol in a few words I would
use the blessing said on the occasion of the new moon:
K'shem sh'ani raked k'neg'dcha v'ayni l'ngoa boch—No
matter how high I reach for you, I cannot touch you.
Sasha spent his youth in pursuit of Tamara, reached for
her, and could never touch her.

At first, when Sasha was a fifth-level Gymnasium
student, still an adolescent feeling for the first trace of a
mustache, he would frequently pass Itzikl Shostepol's
daughter on the stairway. He would stare at her black
eyes, so shiny, gentle, and lovely, which nevertheless
always left him with the impression that she was laughing at him and his red hair, inherited from his pharmacist father. Still, he always had the desire to stop and talk
to her, to become acquainted with her, to chat a while,

discuss a book or just talk about anything at all, as boys and girls will do. But it never seemed to work out, because Tamara was raised in the kind of home in which a girl is taught never to stop and chat with a boy she doesn't know, and her father would certainly disapprove of her getting to know him.

Itzikl Shostepol had lived at No. 13 Vasilchikover Street for many years but was barely acquainted with Solomon Safranovitch except for ordering medicine from him or stopping in for a donation for some worthwhile charity. For Itzikl Shostepol, Solomon Safranovitch had no other name but "The Pharmacist." "Good morning to you, Pharmacist!" "Reb Pharmacist! How about a little donation to a worthy cause?" And having accepted the donation and left the pharmacy, he had nothing more to do with him.

What could he possibly have in common with him when on Shabbos—so Shivka told him—they cooked like every other day of the week, nor did they perform the erev-Yom Kippur rituals. And as for Pesach—may God not punish her for these words, for Shivka Shostepol didn't wish to speak ill of another Jew, but she couldn't help feeling outraged and upset. "After all, Pesach! Such a sacred holiday, Pesach! But what's Pesach to them? Nothing!" She did not say all this too loudly, but one could understand their attitude irked her.

As a kosher Jew hates pork, so did the pharmacist dislike Itzikl, but he never showed his animosity toward him. On the contrary, he was as friendly to him as he was to all the other neighbors. What else could he do? You have to make a living. To himself he called Itzikl Shostepol "God's gonif," "hypocrite," "Yiddash"— phony Jew—and other such names. But to his face he called him in Russian *Gaspodin*—Respected Mr.

Shostepol—and sometimes *Mnagaavozshayem!*—Highly
Esteemed Mr. Shostepol. Why he deserved this honor
even he himself didn't know. During all the years they
had been neighbors the pharmacist had never asked the
slightest favor of Itzikl Shostepol, yet there it was, the
"highly esteemed Mr. Shostepol."

Sasha, the pharmacist's son, was a fine boy and one of
the best students in the Gymnasium. He applied himself
to his studies, read a good deal, and wasn't distracted by
the trivialities as other boys were. But since he had
become aware of Tamara's large lovely eyes, he would
often be lost in yearning, become preoccupied, and
long to see those eyes again and again—until finally
they appeared to him one night in a dream. And
they appeared to him with such intensity and force
that they enveloped him in their splendor and radiance.
They were suffused with such charm and kindliness,
with such longing and warmth that they penetrated into
the depths of his heart, becoming so permanently a
part of his very being that there was no way he
could ever be rid of them no matter how hard he
tried.

Sasha himself could not account for the power compelling him to wait for hours on the stairs in case Itzikl
Shostepol's daughter might appear so that he might
again see those black lovely intelligent eyes. And if he
did meet with her fiery glance, he would at once take to
his heels, running home to his studies, to his books,
where he would again sink deep in thought and again
dream of Itzikl's daughter, of her lithe figure and of her
large black intelligent eyes, and again wait on the stairs
and again meet her and again take to his heels. And so it
went for a long time, until he could bear it no longer
and made up his mind to speak to Itzikl Shostepol's
daughter.

Itzikl Shostepol didn't want his daughter to go to Gymnasium like all the other girls, but he spared no expense in hiring the best tutors and governesses to educate her properly. And the best tutors—as Itzikl saw it—were gentiles, not Jews. A Jewish teacher was, first of all, a heretic and encouraged his students to become dissolute, while a gentile teacher knew only one thing: he was being paid money and so had to teach.

Itzikl Shostepol proceeded on that assumption and took the trouble of paying a visit to the best teacher at the Gymnasium for his advice, to Romanenko himself. As he, Shostepol, had a very gifted daughter, could he, Romanenko, recommend the best tutor for her?

Romanenko heard him out and said, "If you want a good teacher, a dependable one, I can recommend my own son. He is an excellent pedagogue, a former student who quarreled with his professors and is now living at home without a job."

You can be quite certain that if Romanenko had been a Jewish boy, a "former student" at that, Itzikl Shostepol would never have allowed him into his house, but a Jew has respect for a gentile, no matter what he is, so long as he is a gentile.

Our enemies, who don't know much about Jewish life in the Diaspora and who are unacquainted with Diaspora psychology, imagine that a Jew despises a gentile and is wary of him. They are not aware of the secret that whatever is strange to him the Jew considers to be better than his own. If a Jew wants someone to believe what he is saying, he will say, "I heard it from a gentile, not a Jew." They don't realize that the main aspiration of a well-to-do Jew is to be accepted by gentile society and to have the good opinion of gentiles; one gentile compliment is worth a thousand times more than ten thousand Jewish compliments. No other people have such expressions as "our little Jews," "with a Jew it's only good to eat kugel," "Jewish stories," "Jewish mazel," "Jewish superstitions," and other such insulting expressions that could evolve only in a people living for hundreds of years in exile.

When Romanenko, the former student, arrived for Tamara's first lesson, Itzikl Shostepol quickly removed his everyday hat in his honor and donned a round satin yarmulke—after all, he was supposed to be a rich man! And that was the pattern every day: Romanenko came in, the hat came off; Romanenko left, the yarmulke came off.

And Romanenko, the tutor, the former student, did his job well. He studied with Tamara, he read with Tamara, he educated Tamara, fell in love with Tamara, and Tamara fell in love with Romanenko.

Neither Romanenko nor Tamara declared their feelings or even acknowledged them. Theirs was a silent collision of two burning stars swept by tremendous force as they soared in the infinity of their ideals without giving any thought to what they were doing, where they were going, and what the final outcome might be.

Whoever knows the history of the events that took place at that time will understand the real meaning of the words "former student." Young men such as Romanenko were without doubt the finest people in the land. They were warmhearted, possessed of pure minds and high ideals, matched by the will to achieve something good and useful for their many hungry, unfortunate fellow countrymen. In short, Romanenko was not merely a socialist and a revolutionary but was also a leader, an organizer of an entire political circle. And it was such a man who was forced to spend his time at home, and it was he whom Itzikl Shostepol selected as the tutor for his pampered only daughter, Tamara.

How fortunate our Itzikl considered himself to be when he heard from Romanenko himself, from a gentile, that his daughter was not only a good student but already knew a good deal and was herself a good person—all in all she was a model of goodness!

More than once Itzikl Shostepol boasted to his Jewish friends about the wonderful teacher he had engaged, a gentile, and what this gentile teacher had said about his daughter! And he, Itzikl, would see to it that his daughter would continue studying. He wouldn't mind if she were to pass the examination in all eight Gymnasium levels. Attending Gymnasium wasn't at all necessary, but passing the examinations and earning a diploma—why not?

And Itzikl had his way. His daughter didn't attend classes, studied at home—tutored by Romanenko—took the examinations in all eight Gymnasium levels, and brought home a diploma! For our Itzikl Shostepol that was indeed a happy day, a day of triumph. His Tamara had a diploma, had completed all eight levels, and without ever going to class.

"Hah, what do you say to that, Shivka?"

"What should I say?" Shivka answered him. "Now it's time to start thinking about making a match."

"Heh? What? A match, you say? So soon?" Itzikl questioned her, braiding and twisting and tugging at his curly little black beard. "Why are you in such a hurry? Then again, maybe. Maybe you're right, Shivka. Maybe it *is* time to talk about a match."

And Itzikl Shostepol thought about his daughter, how grown-up she had become, an individual, *kayn ayn horeh,* a beautiful woman; everyone said she was a beauty, even the gentiles.

Tamara continued to read books, went on with her studies, meeting daily with her teacher, Romanenko.

Her parents couldn't understand what more there was for her to study. How long must one go on studying? And did the teacher have to keep coming every day? And the father waited for a time and then called Tamara to him and said to her, "My child, what are you and your teacher doing these days?"

"Nothing," the daughter answered. "We read books together, we talk."

"How much longer does this go on? It has to come to an end sometime, no?"

"What has to come to an end?" his daughter asked.

"Learning has to come to an end," her father replied.

"Learning has no end," Tamara said to him.

"Doesn't even the Torah have an end?" her father said jokingly.

"Of course not," Tamara retorted, also jokingly. "I'm just starting at '*mah tovu*.'"

"Just at the beginning?" Her father continued the joke: "When will you come to God?"

"When I finish university and spend a few years working in a clinic and in a hospital, then I will first begin my practical work, which will be for me a new school in which to study."

Itzikl Shostepol was utterly dumbfounded. He was speechless. At first he didn't respond at all to his daughter's plan. Instead he sprang up from his chair, head lowered, and began pacing the room, his hands clasped behind him. After a time he stopped pacing and planted himself in front of his daughter so that their large black eyes opposed each other from beneath lowered brows. Wordless and alert, they glared like two wild animals who are ready to pounce upon each other.

Then the father announced in a resolute voice, "Tamara! You will do exactly as I say!"

To which Tamara answered in the same resolute

voice, "Father! You are mistaken! I will do exactly as *I* want!"

"What? What did you say? Say it again!"

"I will say it ten more times, a hundred more times. I will do as *I* want!"

"So, we'll see!"

"We'll see!"

Nonsense! Itzikl Shostepol was wise enough to realize that these were not the times when one could force a child to do the will of the parents. The times had so changed that everywhere, at least among Jews, parents were satisfied when they weren't forced to do what their children wanted. Itzikl Shostepol personally escorted his daughter to Petersburg, found lodgings for her at a relative's, a printer's wife, went with her to buy books, paper, clothes, and so forth. When the time came to take leave of her, to kiss and part, the father felt like crying, but the daughter took his hand in hers, saying, "Feh, Father, this is unbecoming in you. That's the way an old woman behaves! You can go home in peace. You know your daughter is no longer a child you have to worry about. There is, thank God, the mail carrying letters back and forth. I'll probably come home for the holidays. Have a safe trip and kiss Mother for me."

The entire trip back Itzikl Shostepol sat in the train lost in thought. What's going on here? My daughter— my one and only child, who will have everything I own when I die—why does she have to keep on studying and learning? She has to have a profession, she says, so she can be a self-sufficient person—nnuuu! That's what it comes down to! And who is to blame if not me? It was my crazy idea for her to study, develop herself, become educated. Serves me right!

These were Itzikl Shostepol's thoughts as he twisted

and braided and tugged at his curly little black beard. He comforted himself with the knowledge that his daughter had not gone and done something worse. For instance, how would it have been if Tamara had fallen in love with a shlimazel—someone like the pharmacist's son, who was always underfoot, lurking on the stairs?

And he remembered the redheaded Sasha Safranovitch, who had also gone to study in Petersburg and who, on the trip there, was constantly hovering about, not having the nerve to come too close.

"What's that pharmacist's boy doing here?" Itzikl had asked his daughter, and was told, "He's going to study."

"To study? Everyone is studying. What is he studying?"

"Medicine."

"Together with you?"

"What does he have to do with me?"

Those last words relieved him somewhat. Nevertheless he arrived home in an ugly mood, venting his bitterness on his wife, as is usual when a man comes home upset. A wise wife who knows and understands her husband leaves him alone till the meshugas passes. But Shivka wasn't to be counted among the wise wives. Whatever her heart felt or her mind thought her mouth spoke out. Seeing her husband returning home at last, she met him with "So? What's new?"

"What should be new?"

"How's the child?"

"How should she be?"

"Did you take her to Petersburg?"

"No, I left her along the way."

"Did you get her a place to stay?"

"No, I left her on the sidewalk."

"Why are you so irritable?"

"Don't bother me!"

A wise wife who knows and understands her husband bites her lip and remains silent when she has been belittled. But Shivka was, as already noted, not one of those wise wives. She waited a while and started on another topic. "What do you think of our neighbor?"

"What neighbor?"

"The pharmacist."

"Why do you ask?"

"Yesterday he met me on the stairs and he said to me, 'Your husband's off to Petersburg?' So I said, 'He's off to Petersburg.' Said he, 'He's taking your daughter?' Said I, 'Taking my daughter.' 'I,' said he, 'sent my son off by himself.'"

"That really makes me happy!" said Itzikl to his wife, glaring at her with those large black eyes. "Why are you telling me all this?"

"No special reason," said Shivka. "Just like this. And afterward he said to me—the pharmacist, that is— 'My son is acquainted with your daughter.'"

"That makes me even happier! Why do I have to know all this?" shouted Itzikl.

"Why are you shouting? Well, you've just come home from a trip, so I'm telling you, that's all."

"Did I ask you?"

"Look at how he's lost his temper!"

"Leave me alone! And stop pestering me!"

Itzikl Shostepol grabbed his umbrella and ran out of the apartment, smack into the pharmacist. One can't be so rude as not to reply to a "Good morning" with a "Good day," and so when the neighbor said, "How are you?" he had to pause and say, "Thank you, how are you?" And that's how, without Itzikl's wanting it, a conversation ensued between our two neighbors.

Pharmacist: When did you arrive back from Petersburg?
Itzikl: Today.
Pharmacist: Took your daughter to school?
Itzikl: Took my daughter to school.
Pharmacist: She's studying medicine?
Itzikl: Studying medicine.
Pharmacist: Mine I sent off by himself.
Itzikl: By himself.
Pharmacist: A son is not a daughter.
Itzikl: Not a daughter.
Pharmacist: Mine knows yours very well.
Itzikl: Very well. Please excuse me, I have no time.

And Itzikl Shostepol went off, more furious than before, thinking, What does this pharmacist want from me? Why is he bothering to tell me his son knows my daughter? Does he have something in mind? Can he be hinting at a match? A fine in-law, Solomon the pharmacist, ha-ha-ha-ha!"

Itzikl Shostepol's somber thoughts emerged in a bitter laugh. He was soon faced with a new annoyance in the form of Lippa.

The wood hauler, Lippa, had found out that Itzikl had just returned from Petersburg, so he came over as quickly as he could to see if by any chance Itzikl had encountered his daughter and might have regards from her.

"Sholom aleichem to you, Reb Itzikl, I've been chasing after you for half an hour," said Lippa the wood hauler, stroking his broom beard.

"What's on your mind?" Shostepol asked him.

"I wanted to ask you if you met my daughter Masha there?"

"What Masha?"

"My daughter Masha!"

"Where would I meet her?"

"There, in Petersburg, together with your daughter. She's a good friend."

"Who?"

"My daughter. Masha is her name. She knows your daughter very well. Do you know who introduced them?"

"Who?"

"The teacher."

"Which teacher?"

"Romanenko. He's a regular Party man."

"What's a Party man?"

Lippa the wood hauler stroked his broom beard and glanced around on all sides, then spoke in a whisper, "He's a Tzotzelist!"

"A what?"

"A Tzotzelist, belongs to the Tzotzelists." He looked around again and continued in a whisper, "He made them all Tzotzelists, mine and yours."

"Mine? Out of the question! Excuse me, I have no time."

And Itzikl Shostepol ran off like a madman, as if demons were chasing him. What a nuisance! he thought. Everybody is boasting that they know her. Nu! They know her. Mazel tov! Let them know her.

But that wasn't the entire truth. A worm had entered his heart and was gnawing at him. He truly resented the fact that any shlimazel who knew his daughter could talk so openly about her. But the worst poison had been administered by that big-bearded Jew Lippa, with his "Tzotzelism." Actually, Itzikl had picked up hints of all this before. He remembered hearing his daughter dropping "the organization," "constitution," "self-sufficiency," and other such words into their conversation when they would discuss matters, but he, foolish father that he was, instead of listening to her would look at her eyes with pride, his chest swelling, thinking, She has a man's head on her shoulders. What will she grow up to be? It's a pity she wasn't born a boy.

And the proud father would build castles in air about his beloved Tamara, imagining that a millionaire such as the rich Polyakov from Petersburg had come to pay him a visit expressing his interest in marrying his daughter. The daughter had sent him to her father, and he, the father, was entertaining Polyakov in the large parlor, sitting with him at the small round table, one chair right next to the other, and they were talking of railroads, of bridges, of sugar factories, of lumber footage, of rails, and of anything else that came into their heads, until they came to the real purpose of the discussion—to his Tamara.

"I have heard, Herr Shostepol, that you have a very gifted daughter," Polyakov said, toying with his watch fob.

"Where did you hear this? As far away as Petersburg?" Itzikl exclaimed, his heart almost leaping out with joy and pride.

"Good news," Polyakov said, "travels far. I've already seen her, talked with her too. She pleases me very much. I am, you must know, Polyakov's son, and as for my estate, thank God—"

"Oh," Shostepol interrupted him, "we've heard about your estate, may it happen to me. The main question is this: Is she—I mean my daughter—is she pleased with you?"

And Itzikl Shostepol beamed, his heart swelled with happiness, with pride, with good fortune! Imagine having Polyakov for a son-in-law! He was worth at least thirty million! He could tell the whole city, the whole world, to go to hell!!!

These were the sweet dreams of the foolish father, and these dreams were suddenly dashed to bits in a single day, in the twinkling of an eye, in that moment when Tamara declared that her only ambition was to study medicine, to become a doctor, to practice medicine, become a useful servant to mankind, and other such strange ideas. What sort of match could she make then? Marriage? She would never speak of such things, nor would she even hear of them.

On the other hand, paternal love sought justification for his child's behavior. He wished to be her protector, and he thus found this consolation: There's no other Tamara like my Tamara! There are no others as capable, as beautiful, as bright, as dear, and as loyal as my daughter! And he reminded himself of how she had bade him farewell and what she had told him, and he felt somewhat comforted. He drove away all the dark thoughts and all the irrelevant talk and all those bothersome people who kept showing up. He allowed himself to see a ray of hope: she might change. Why couldn't she meet someone like Polyakov there, in Petersburg? And then her whole plan would be turned upside down—head down, feet up. If only the One Above would want it so!

Don't fret! Don't fret at all! Faith! God in heaven, faith! Hope! Confidence in the Lord! He, if he wills it, he can do anything!

3

Masha Bashevitch

Lippa Bashevitch the wood-hauler was a hardworking Jew who supplied homes with wood, from which he made a living, raised children and educated them.

"Raised children and educated them"—that's easy to say. But considering his circumstances, if you will permit me to say so, how could a wretched pauper like Lippa Bashevitch raise and educate children when his mind was always taken up with the struggle to earn a crust of bread for himself, for his wife and children, a struggle that was hardly successful? The impoverished Bashevitch tried everything, going from house to house offering to sell a full load of wood, a whole klafter, measuring three and a quarter by three and a quarter, for a mere fifty-two vershuk. And it could even be paid off in installments, only a ruble a week. Do you hear? Have you ever heard of such a thing? In installments!

In spite of all these inducements, once he had succeeded in finding a customer and they had agreed on a price and the wood had been ordered from him, had been measured out three times in the width, and his son-in-law had checked the measurements (the son-in-law was a young man who was good at figures, a mathematician who knew algebra), and a neighbor was also asked to double-check, and then, with God's help, the wood had been cut up, stacked, and was already being used to heat the house for a week—then, when they came to collect the first ruble, they were greeted by complaints from the woman of the house, complaints that darkened his life.

"A fine load of wood you gave me! May my enemies be so lucky! You call that wood? Till you live to see even a spark, your eyes can fall out of your head!"

"What are you talking about, Madamenyu, may you remain strong and healthy," the poor wood hauler pleaded. "It's gold, not wood! It's real aged hardwood, not just scrap or softwood!"

"You're a strange man," her husband broke in. "We're telling you that the wood is damp—and damp wood won't burn—and you insist that the wood is dry!"

"The wood must have come from a green tree," volunteered the son-in-law, the one who was good at figures, the mathematician who knew algebra.

The miraculous strokes of good fortune that Jews experienced in that crowded, dark, dismal, filthy ghetto where the Diaspora had flung them together helter-skelter were so great and wondrous that each individual could have told a story to rival the exodus from Egypt. Each could have described how God had dealt with him, how he had survived a year and then another year, raised and married off one child, and another child, and yet another child—miracle upon miracle!

Lippa Bashevitch would have more to tell than any-one. Eight children God had granted him, and all eight were gifted. They knew everything and were informed about everything. You might ask when and where they had had the chance to study. Did they ever receive any education at all? Only to the extent that the father him-self used to teach them a little at night. Did they ever have a teacher? Only to the extent that one assisted the other. And in spite of that, as fate would have it, they had all entered Gymnasium, studied well, and so ex-celled that the anti-Semitic teacher, the elder Roma-nenko, managed not only to exempt them from tuition but furnished them with clothing and shoes, because Lippa's children went half naked and barefoot till the age of fifteen.

If Lippa Bashevitch had had to depend on others to say a good word about his children he would have had to wait a long time. He had a daughter Masha about whom he said, "Since God had created this Masha, He has never created another such. The way she accom-plishes her chores at home—golden hands! Not to men-tion her studies—the highest grades! Have you ever seen her diploma? You haven't? I haven't shown it to you? Here, I'll show it to you, then you'll first *see* a diploma! And by herself, all by herself. I'm telling you, this is a Masha sent from heaven, blessed by God! A one-in-a-million Masha!"

That's how Lippa Bashevitch crowed to all his neigh-bors and acquaintances, boring them to tears with his Masha. And needless to say, when Masha finished Gymnasium and brought home a gold medal, her proud father, poor as ever, almost went out of his mind and almost drove all his neighbors and acquaintances and even strangers out of *their* minds. He would stop every-one, show off the medal, and tell of Masha's outstanding scholarship, how she had impressed the director and the teachers, and how proficient she was at home, teaching the younger children, and what an excellent essay she had sent to the minister that she, Masha herself, had written. And without a moment's pause he would pull out the essay and recite it in a lofty voice, rising and falling in tone: *"Yevo visakaprevoshoditelstvo Gospodinu Ministru naradnaha prosveshtshenya . . ."*—His Most Esteemed Sir Minister of Public Education . . .

The neighbors were relieved to be rid of Lippa Bashevitch when his daughter Masha went away to Petersburg. Now, they reckoned, he would stop pestering them about his Masha. But they were sadly mistaken. They now had to hear every word of Masha's correspondence to her parents from Petersburg. Remarkable letters! She was working very hard, mending laundry to earn the bare necessities, and was studying medicine. She wrote of a new life that would soon prevail in all the land, a life of freedom, of equality based on a constitution. In every letter she spoke of some sort of constitution; it got to the point where the neighbors gave Lippa the nickname "Constitutzia." Instead of Lippa Bashevitch they began to call him Lippa Constitutzia. People made jokes about Lippa's daughter and her constitution. But Masha, for whom it was no joke, worked incessantly for the constitution and believed that someday—if not today, then tomorrow—they would have that wonderful long-awaited, hoped-for constitution! "They will *have* to give it to us," Masha argued. "A deluge of blood will flow! The deluge will drown the sinful earth and rinse away all the evil, and the skies will clear and the sun will shine and it will become light in all the land!"

So preached Masha Bashevitch at every opportunity among the youth and among the workers, becoming well known in certain circles and beloved by the common people. "Our Masha"—that's what she was called in those circles, and many were prepared to follow her through fire and flood to the very ends of the earth.

No letter carrier in the great city of Petersburg walked as many miles a day as our Masha Bashevitch. After awakening early in the morning and dispatching at least ten letters to various friends about various matters, she would walk miles from the edge of the city to the Institute, from the Institute again a fair distance to the Dyeshavke market, where one could always find the cheapest lunch, and from there again several miles to work at the factory, and from there to friends, from the friends back home to the edge of town, all on foot. To use the public transportation would require "Rothschild's fortune and Korach's riches," Masha said, and she tore through Petersburg like a racehorse, not allowing herself to cease her work for a moment.

What Masha Bashevitch's work consisted of no one except the Party and her closest friends knew or needed to know; it was political conspiracy. But the police knew about all of her activities and exactly what she had been doing, and they were searching for her intensively; thus far they had been unable to find her.

But there was one man who had sworn to trap her. He was the notorious spy named Yashka Vorona.

4

Yashka Vorona

On his papers it said "Yaakov Vladimorivitch Voronin, thirty-two years old." His real name was Yankel Voroner, and he came from a small town in Grodno Province. His life story is interesting, and we relate it here as briefly as possible.

His father a teacher . . . His mother a baker . . . Starved till the age of five . . . From the age of five helped deliver food to cheder children, earned a groschen, bought a bagel from his mother for supper . . . Delivered Purim *shalach-mones* . . . Went barefoot summers till age thirteen . . . After his Bar Mitzvah refused to say prayers . . . Beaten by his father, who broke his arm . . . Ran away to Grodno . . . Slept in the streets . . . Learned Russian and mathematics from a madman . . . Stole a Gemorah from a shul, was imprisoned for stealing half a loaf of bread . . . Ran away to the Mir Yeshiva . . . Masqueraded as an

Orthodox Jew, prayed from morning to night . . . Was fed by charitable Jews . . . Stole rolls from the table of his hosts . . . Was caught smoking in the bathroom on Shabbos . . . Was flogged . . . Ran away to Bialystok . . . Became a teacher . . . Charged a gulden a week to teach two hours a day . . . Starved . . . Married a girl who was stone-deaf . . . Received fifty-five rubles dowry . . . Bought himself a pair of boots (his first pair of boots!) . . . Ran away to Vilna . . . Passed the sixth-level examination . . . Fell in with thieves . . . Wrote Yiddish dramas . . . Tried to sell them to a publisher . . . Publisher proposed they be bought by weight: two gulden a pound . . . Tore up the dramas, wrote a satire on the publisher . . . Showed it to friends . . . All were delighted . . . Sent it off to a Yiddish periodical . . . Never saw it again . . . Fell in love with a girl . . . An ugly business . . . Wanted to drown himself in the Velikaya . . . Was informed his father dead, his mother starving . . . Vowed to study law . . . Worked for a pharmacist . . . Spent two years there . . . Sent his mother money—a ruble a week, two rubles on holidays . . . Pharmacist accused him of handing out free perfume to poor girls . . . Had an affair with the pharmacist's wife . . . Ran off to Petersburg . . . Wanted to study medicine . . . Starved . . . Tried to get an interview with Baron Guinzburg . . . Stood for hours in the cold . . . Attracted the attention of police . . . Was arrested . . . Was to be shipped with convoy of convicts to Grodno . . . Converted . . . Gave up hope of introduction to Baron Guinzburg . . . Could not send money anymore to his mother . . . Went hungry himself . . . Got a job in an arsenal . . . Attended lectures at the university . . . Participated in all meetings . . . Became acquainted with all the students and workers . . . Concealed the fact he had converted . . .

Was involved in a dynamite plot . . . Almost got to visit Siberia . . . Compromised himself . . . Informed on a few comrades, quickly released . . . Wanted to hang himself . . . Was offered work as a spy . . . Overjoyed to receive his first hundred . . . Fell in love with a gentile washerwoman . . . Had two children . . . Served loyally . . . Authorities highly pleased with him . . . Bought his own house . . . Kept advancing . . . Suspected by some of the workers . . . Feared for his life . . . Tried to save his skin . . . Had the honor several times to report personally to highest authorities . . . Won assignment in Warsaw . . . Accomplished mission in best form . . . Won an award and permanent post in Petersburg . . . Would be completely happy if workers didn't threaten his life . . .

That is the up-to-date biography of Yashka Vorona.

Yashka Vorona had to admit that the job of finding the hidden Masha was his most difficult, and he would never forget her as long as he lived! He suspected a girl with short hair who once left a meeting with a crowd late at night, stopping every so often to have a discussion (it was during those happy times when three people could talk together freely in the streets without fear). After leaving the group this girl took a droshky and asked to be taken to one of the dark streets of the great city of Petersburrg. Naturally Yashka quickly took another droshky and followed her to her destination, where she stopped, paid the driver, got out, rang the doorbell, and entered the courtyard. Our agent waited a while, rang for the watchman, entered the courtyard, showed the man his credentials, and asked to be shown the tenant register. Yashka leafed through the register several times and stopped at the name Miriam Gitl Bashevitch, living with a former resident of Orsha, Moishe Malkin.

"Ah??? Malkin? . . . A familiar name. I should learn something from him."

57

5

The Little Commune

Malkin had for a long time been known to the police because of his finagling to obtain residences for Jews in neighborhoods where they were not allowed and through his constant applying for permits. Nothing could stop him—neither being arrested nor being sent off to prison. Malkin stubbornly decided once and for all that the town of Orsha was too small for him and he wanted to be a Petersburger. And he succeeded. He brought with him from Orsha a "document" stating he was a businessman, a shoe-polish maker, and settled in Petersburg as a shoe-polish maker.

There were two forces working in favor of Malkin's becoming a Petersburg resident: one force drove him from Orsha, because there was nothing to do there; the other force drew him to Petersburg, because he had heard that in Petersburg Jews were becoming rich, enormously rich, from the war (this was the time of the

Russo-Japanese War). But Malkin was too late. Because of his shady dealings with illegal residences and because he had been away in prison, he had missed the most prosperous times, the golden times, and had arrived in Petersburg when they were already talking of peace, and our shoe-polish maker had gone through a great deal of trouble for nothing.

Malkin would have starved to death if his wife hadn't come to his aid with her great talent for cooking fish and baking challah. He opened a low-cost pension, hung out a shingle, and prospered. In a short time, by word of mouth, people found out that at Malkin's you could get delicious fish and fresh challah every day and cheaply. And Malkin's rooms, which were located right under the roof, on the very top floor, were soon occupied by regular boarders, young people of different professions, or rather, without any professions at all, who were called "proletarian intelligentsia." Such people would prefer to be doing whatever was useful—working, toiling, anything to earn a piece of bread—not for money, mind you, but enough to keep body and soul together in order to be able to further their great work in behalf of the sacred ideas that had brought them all together, right under the roof of Malkin the shoe-polish maker.

These are the boarders who lived at Malkin's, under the roof.

Meyer Gridell: Twenty-two years old, a Bundist. Studied in three Gymnasia; didn't finish any of them because of mathematics, which for him was a bourgeois joke. Quarreled with his parents. Ran away to Petersburg, registered as a typesetter, entered the university. Of short stature, swarthy, pockmarked face, nearsighted.

Chaim Broida: Thirty-four years old. Had been a teacher. Taught himself languages. Read a great deal. A fierce anti-Zionist and antinationalist. Secretly read banned periodical *Hashalach*. Registered as a tailor. Only God and he alone knew on what he lived. Tall, slender, with a hoarse voice, appeared to be a candidate for tuberculosis, but perhaps not.

Mischa Berezniak (Real name Moishe Fiedler): Around forty years old. Escaped from Siberia. Had two degrees. Exceptionally strong. Talked with a droning voice. Very much wanted by the police. Made his living by singing in a church choir every Sunday. Hard to tell he was a Jew. Large, hairy, looked like a Russian priest. Had a wild temper.

Nissel Avrutis: Nineteen-year-old youngster. Never studied anywhere. Possessed rare gifts. Published poems in the best Russian newspapers, signed himself "Kolivri." A fiery anarchist. Registered as a dyer. Pale as a girl, with soft cheeks.

Etka Vayrach: Twenty-four years old. A Litvak from Bobruisk. Registered as a wigmaker. Completed Gymnasium. Studying dentistry. Made her living gluing cardboard cartons. Dark complexion, quite attractive. Fiery-eyed.

Chava Vahl: Twenty-one years old. Came from an aristocratic family. Her father boasted his ancestor was the Jewish-Polish king Shaul Vahl. Threw over a rich suitor. Taught herself massage. Registered as a hatmaker. A dangerous revolutionary. Not attractive.

Masha Bashevitch: We already know.

Now we must introduce you to Malkin's three older boys. One should say "men" rather than "boys" because they were three tall, healthy brutes, with stout legs and strong arms, who worked hard and ate heartily. They had the kind of appetite that a millionaire could not support. One developed an appetite by merely watching them eat. Seventeen holiday feasts,

eighteen wedding suppers, a hundred banquets, din-
ners, and buffets given by multimillionaires couldn't
compare with one weekday's meals of that proletarian-
intelligentsia bunch upstairs under the roof. No one
stood on ceremony. No one sat at the head of the table.
They sat and talked and ate, all on the same footing, like
partners, like a commune.

With time it actually did become something of a commune, thanks to the new boarder, Masha Bashevitch.
When Masha Bashevitch came to her first meal to ar-
range her room and board she immediately felt at home.
After meeting the group and learning each one's name,
Masha tossed off her hat and coat, and, dinner over, she
rolled up her sleeves and started helping Frau Malkin
wash the dishes. Malkin himself tried to protest, but
Masha cut him off.

"It's none of your business! If I have the time, I'll help
you. If I don't have the time, you'll help *me*. Here, for
example, my shoe is torn, do you see? Be so kind, Herr
Malkin, take my shoe to the shoemaker. I saw a shoemaker in your courtyard. Ask him what he wants to
repair it, and while you're at it, I would appreciate it if
you would pay him, as I'm short of cash today."

Several minutes later Masha heard a child crying from
behind the stove and she turned to Frau Malkin and
said, "Is that one of yours? So show me that crybaby
and we'll see what the matter is." And Masha took the
child on her lap, gave him the nickname of "Pempek,"
for his fat tummy, bounced him and jounced him and
danced with him till the crying baby stuck his pink little
tongue out, showed six newly cut teeth, and laughed
gleefully.

"Why are you sitting like clods, with your hands
folded?" Masha shouted at the two girls who were
studying dentistry and massage.

"What should we be doing?" the girls answered with a questioning laugh.

"What should you be doing! Take an automobile drive through the Nevski! There's a broom—take it and sweep out the rooms."

As one could imagine, that first night at supper all of them wanted to impress Masha Bashevitch with their own liberal ideas and their fine oratory. A discussion ensued about principal economic issues, and the words poured forth: Karl Marx, LaSalle, proletariat, Koitski, class struggle . . .

"Be quiet, all of you!" shouted Masha, covering her ears. "If you want to carry on a debate like people, not like geese, you have to do it according to parliamentary rules—elect a president and ask to be recognized. This time I am your president. Herr Berezniak, you have the floor!"

And that's how a small commune evolved at Malkin's, and its leader was Masha Bashevitch.

6

The Bird Shot At and Missed

It was not yet dark, and not all the streetlights had been turned on, when the small commune located right under the roof of Malkin's apartment began gathering one by one to exchange with one another the day's happenings. Each one had a bundle of news to untie—one about a secret meeting, one about a fight over the workers, another about a new strike that was being planned —and each one wanted to be heard first. But Malkin, the landlord himself, cut in, shouting to be heard over the others.

"Do you know what I have to tell you, friends? Just listen to me and I'll tell you something really funny. First of all, I'm older than all of you. I'm not even mentioning the fact that I'm the landlord here, because I know the word 'landlord' means very little to you. And second of all, I promise you, you will have a good laugh!"

"If we'll have a good laugh, Herr Malkin, then you can go first, you can have the floor."

Obviously these words were spoken by Masha Bashevitch, who all this time was sitting preoccupied and troubled, drumming her fingers on the table—a sure sign she wasn't in a good mood. And the landlord Malkin started to tell his story.

"This morning, when all of you had vanished as salt dissolves in water and I remained all alone with little Pempek here"—he gestured toward his small son, who was sitting on the masseuse's lap, pulling her nose—"the door opened and in came a deliveryman carrying books and sat himself down to chat with me. As usually happens, little Pempek here didn't let anyone get a word in. To make a long story short, it turns out he is a sympathizer, and a committed one too, selling banned books. And while he was at it he confided to me that the girl who had broken into the typesetter's and printed those proclamations—Masha is her name—was his daughter. So? Didn't I say you would have a good laugh?"

"So? What did you tell him?" asked Masha.

"What *could* I tell him?" said Malkin. "I told him he was really a big liar. He tried to contradict me and to convince me that it was indeed his daughter's work, and this really annoyed me. So I disabused him and revealed to him the secret that this Masha was a different Masha and that I knew her and that she was living here in my house."

As if an angry bee had stung her, Masha Bashevitch sprang up! She slapped her hands together and cried out to Malkin, "What have you done? You're really a child, an overgrown child, and a foolish child at that! Who asked you to prattle on with that loose tongue of yours? Ach, Malkin! Malkin!"

And Masha began pacing back and forth, storming through the apartment, muttering angrily and wringing her hands. The entire commune and Malkin himself were terrified by her; as long as they had known Masha Bashevitch they had never seen her so distraught and upset. All attempts to calm or soothe her were of no avail. Masha Bashevitch didn't allow herself to be mollified. And it was Malkin who was the object of her rage.

"What right did you have to discuss things that are none of your business with a total stranger you don't know at all? I am convinced he is one of them, the police. Our doorman mentioned to me this morning that after I came home last night, some character was looking for someone—he wasn't sure whether it was for me or another woman. Children, do you know what I will tell you? I'm going to have to move to other lodgings, and immediately. Don't try to talk me out of it, stop making long faces and sad speeches. Better help me pack my bags, and if one of you would be so kind, please tell the doorman to cross my name off the register and tell him I've gone to Vilna. If they want to find me, at least let them go out of their way. Take care, little Pempek, give me your dirty little face. I hope you grow up to be at least a bit smarter than your father. Adieu!"

One's own sister would not be so warmly sent off as Masha was by the little commune. They were all moved and downcast at this unexpected turn of events. Frau Malkin couldn't control herself and burst into tears. And the two female boarders, the dentist and the masseuse, were ready to accompany her, but Masha wouldn't have it.

When she was already out the door, she turned around to face the commune and said to them: "What else have I forgotten to tell you, children? Oh, yes. If you should hear that I've been arrested—who can tell?—don't any of you dare to visit me. Things are getting hotter. Get rid of any evidence as you would get rid of chometz before Pesach—any scrap of a letter, any piece of paper, a proclamation, a pamphlet. Burn them. Whoever feels he needn't remain here had better get out as soon as possible. Take care of yourselves, all of you! Be well, little Pempek, you I will miss."

As could have been predicted, a heated debate erupted among the members of the commune immediately after Masha's departure. Some were highly critical of Masha's leaving and going into hiding; others defended her and got to work burning letters and pamphlets. Malkin's sons helped with the task, and Frau Malkin was happy to be saving wood. Even little Pempek enjoyed the fire, never taking his eyes off it, as if it were burning for his sake alone.

The fire in the stove had long been dead and the ashes from the burned papers had long ago been swept out by Frau Malkin. The remaining members of the commune had each gone to his corner to rest from the work and worry of that day. Only Malkin and his wife sat together next to little Pempek's crib, worrying about where the following day's grocery money would come from. The husband asked the wife and the wife asked the husband, "Where can we get some money?" "It's not good!" Malkin said. "Not good," Frau Malkin repeated, and at that very moment there was a knock on the door, and another knock, and still another, each one louder and more insistent than the previous one.

"Who's there?" asked Malkin.

"Friends," a voice answered from the other side of the door.

"What do you think it can be, a raid?" Malkin asked

his wife, but there was no time for an answer, because before Frau Malkin could open her mouth to reply the door burst open and in came the visitors—the chief of police, several security police, and an officer between them. Terrified, Malkin sat frozen at the table, while Frau Malkin remained by the crib.

"*Zarastvoy, golubchik*—How are you, my dear friend?" the chief of police said to Malkin, whom he had seen more than once in his local precinct office. "How's business?"

Malkin was so stunned he couldn't open his mouth. The local policemen, the security police officers, went about doing their work—they woke up the entire commune and dragged them out of their beds half naked. A soldier stood alongside each one and an interrogation began.

"Masha Bashevitch!" called out an officer, still a young man not yet out of his teens, with two fine curly muttonchops growing on his cheeks à la Pushkin. "Which one of you here is Masha Bashevitch?"

"Masha Bashevitch is not here," Malkin forced himself to say at last.

"What do you mean, she's not here?"

"She's gone."

If someone had thrown a bomb he could not have created a greater effect or have surprised them more than with the news that the one they had been sure of finding was gone.

"Your bird has flown the coop!" the officer with the Pushkin muttonchops said with a bitter little smile to a man who was standing unnoticed near the door dressed in an overcoat of a nondescript color—it was hard to say whether it was gray or brown or yellowish. It would be easier to say it was all three colors at once. All this time the unnoticed person in the three-colored overcoat had been standing on the side like someone who had been called in as a witness. But upon hearing that Masha Bashevitch was not there this man suddenly came to life, went over to the table, looked around angrily through his ash-tinted spectacles, his face frozen, his hands trembling. He went right up to Malkin, looked right into his eyes, and with a quiet but intense voice said to him in Yiddish, "Malkin! Where is Masha Bashevitch? I know that you know. It will be healthier for all of you if you tell the truth."

Malkin recognized his guest of the previous morning, the deliveryman.

It was Yashka Vorona.

7

Masha Seeks a Refuge

When Masha Bashevitch left Malkin's small commune right under the roof, she took her bag, a small felt valise held together with a rope, hailed a droshky, and asked to be taken to one of the outlying streets of greater Petersburg. Since it was a long drive, Masha, as was her habit, engaged in conversation with the coachman, a strong, healthy Orlovsker peasant with the face of a bear. She discovered that he owned a bit of property in Orlovsk Province which didn't provide him with so much as a crust of bread, and so he was forced to be a coachman, his wife had to take in laundry, and his children—ach, the children! He had three sons and a daughter, and one of the sons, the eldest, a reservist, had been killed in Manchuria and another had just joined the army that year.

"Why so many soldiers?" Masha asked him. "Are you providing the Russian Army with soldiers?"

"What can one do?" the coachman answered her. "They ask and we have to give."

The coachman turned his face to her, trying to see to whom he was speaking, whether she might be an informer. But Masha's face told him she was no informer, and on the coachman's face there appeared a grimace that could be interpreted as a smile. He felt free to speak to her, telling her he was not a dim ignoramus as she might suppose but that he was also aware of what was going on in the world. He himself was illiterate, but others read pamphlets to him. Sylvester read to him and explained what they meant. Who was Sylvester? Sylvester was a worker from an iron foundry who shared his living quarters with him. Sylvester told him what was going on at the foundries. They were planning a strike. Even he and his horse would have to go on strike if Father Gapon told them to.

"Who is this Gapon?" Masha asked him in order to find out how well informed the coachman was about what was going on at the foundries.

"Father Gapon," the coachman explained in his own language, "is the priest who was sent to wage war against that black evil spirit, the Antichrist, who has stolen into our country and refuses to leave. No matter how much he is smoked out with incense, no matter how many prayers and curses and pleas and oaths have been heaped on him, yet he refuses to budge, that black spirit, that Antichrist, may he perish from the plague!"

With these words he inflicted on his horse what he wished to inflict on the Antichrist. Masha wanted to find out from this poor soul exactly who he thought this Antichrist was.

"The devil knows!" he answered her. "I think he must come from the Jews."

"Why the Jews?" Masha asked him, astounded.

"Where else if not from the Jews?" the peasant replied with authority. "Everything is because of the Jews. Isn't the war because of the Jews?"

"How do you know that?"

"I *don't* know, but I believe it."

Masha was faced with the task of enlightening him about Gapon, the Antichrist, the Jews, and who had really caused the war. And a difficult bit of work it was; woodchopping was much easier! Nevertheless she was satisfied with her work, because when they arrived at her destination and she paid the coachman for the hour and a half ride, a broad, simple smile appeared on his bearlike face which seemed to express "Now it's all as plain as day!"

They had driven up to a high, gray-painted outside wall, and Masha rang the bell on the door at the entrace. A watchman appeared wearing a white apron and a white badge on his hat. Masha learned from him that the person she was looking for had been arrested and she could not stay there because the landlord had told him not to rent any rooms to students or young women. "Better to let the rooms remain empty," he had said, "or burn them to the ground before the police accuse me of harboring a nest of students, thieves, crooks, and socialists in my place!"

Poor Masha had to pick up her felt valise and look for another place to stay three streets away. The doorbell was answered by a woman wearing a red kerchief with green flowers—the watchman's wife apparently—who told her in a singsong voice to leave as soon as possible, because the whole neighborhood was crawling with police. They were looking for someone.

Obviously our heroine had to make a sharp about-face and quit the area at once, because she was not about

71

to let the police stand in the way of her mission; she had much, much more to do! Suddenly (all good ideas come suddenly) a good idea came to her. Tamara! Tamara Shostepol!

Masha Bashevitch and Tamara Shostepol, though they had been friends from the same city and had graduated from the same Gymnasium, hardly saw each other—not because there were any bad feelings between them but for reasons neither could explain. In her heart Masha admitted she disliked Tamara's bourgeois parents and their bourgeois home. Masha remembered the strong impression Tamara's home had made on her whenever she visited. Tamara's mother would serve her a glass of tea as if it were costing her her last cent. What's to be done? Sometimes you *do* have to serve a guest a glass of tea! And every time the maid forgot to add sugar Tamara's mother would curse her for forgetting.

As for her father, Itzikl Shostepol, she truly despised him. She remembered how once, having come to see Tamara and not finding her at home, she had met the father at the door.

"Who is this girl?" Itzikl had asked his wife, scratching himself under his collar.

"A friend of Tamara's," the wife had answered, not wishing to refer to her by name. Masha was in the sixth-level Gymnasium at the time and could already win an argument with smarter people than Itzikl Shostepol. She said to him proudly, "I am Lippa's daughter."

"What Lippa?"

"Lippa Bashevitch," Masha answered him.

"What Bashevitch?" Itzikl asked again, not removing his hand from his collar.

"The wood hauler," Tamara's mother volunteered. Itzikl turned his back on Masha, and Masha left there in a rage, vowing never to visit Tamara again. But not long after, she ran into Tamara, who insisted she visit, and she talked to her so long that she persuaded her to change her mind.

Once they met in Petersburg at a meeting, and Tamara reprimanded Masha for not coming to visit her. To this Masha replied, "Why don't you come to visit *me?*" But then she realized what she had said and quickly stopped herself. "Besides, you can't come to my place."

"Why?"

"Because Malkin's residence, where I live, is too small for you."

That hurt Tamara's feelings, so she made a *point* of paying her a visit, met Malkin and the whole proletariat bunch, even carried on a discussion with the members of the commune, who all fell in love with her, from the youngest, Avrutis, to the eldest, the former Siberian exile, Berezniak. Tamara liked them all, even the two women of the commune, Etka and Chava.

"Now I hope you will visit me too," said Tamara to Masha.

"At the first opportunity," replied Masha, but no sooner had Tamara left than she forgot about her. She remembered Tamara's invitation only at that moment when she was walking the streets of the great city of Petersburg, bag in hand, seeking a refuge.

After walking several more miles our heroine paused at a brown outside wall and rang the doorbell. Responding to the bell was a small barefooted shikseh with large beads around her neck and a ready smile on her face. Masha handed her the bag and asked her what her name was.

"They call me Masha," the little shikseh with the large beads said, laughing.

"If that's so, we have two Mashas here," Masha

Bashevitch said to the little Masha and asked to be taken to Miss Shostepol's room.

"Who's there?" a man's voice called from the next room.

"It's me!" Masha Bashevitch answered him as she unpacked her bag and made herself at home in Tamara's room.

"Who is 'me'? the same man's voice asked again, and not receiving an answer, the man himself appeared, a forty-year-old, sleepy-eyed and disheveled, without an undershirt and wearing a buttoned-up kind of vest, without suspenders, so that his trousers kept slipping down and he had to hold them up with both hands at his belly, yanking them up frequently. At the same time he had to keep adjusting his pince-nez, which refused to stay put on his nose in spite of the fact that it was a hooked Jewish nose. Apparently it was the fault of the spectacles—not of the nose—or perhaps of the owner of the nose, who looked as if he were an absentminded character, one of those poor souls who are always exhausted and disorganized, who start twenty thousand projects and never finish them.

Seeing an unfamiliar visitor in Tamara's bedroom, the sleepy-eyed man with the drooping trousers sprang back, and bending down as far as his spectacles would allow him to, he asked the banal question, "With whom do I have the honor?" He had a mild speech impediment (instead of "r" it came out "kh").

"The honor is not so great." Masha answered him bluntly, as was her manner, and went about her work—putting away her handkerchiefs, combs and brushes, pillowcases, and little collars as if she were at home. "I'm a hometown friend of Tamara's. My name is Masha Bashevitch."

The name "Masha Bashevitch" went through the

sleepy-eyed man like an electric current. A friendly smile spread over his entire face. He became another person! He clasped her hand and held onto it all the while he spoke, and he spoke at great length without pausing, connecting one subject with the next so cleverly that it was impossible to interrupt him unless one were to leave in the middle of a sentence or shout louder than he. Those who knew him did exactly that— they had no other choice.

"Are you *the* Masha Bashevitch? Ay-ay-ay! When Tamara comes she will jump for joy! We hear about you every day, ten times a day! You are a heroine! Not everyone can do what you are doing. We all have to learn from you. We are children, schoolchildren compared to you! My name is Abram Markovitch. Everyone knows Abram Markovitch! My profession is painting, but I am also a bit of a poet, a vegetarian, and a Tolstoyan. What do I think of Tolstoy? I think very highly of him. You probably think he is a greater poet than a philosopher? I don't agree with you!"

Whether Masha Bashevitch agreed with Abram Markovitch's opinion of Tolstoy or not was another matter, but that she had to remove her hand from his was obvious, and this she did in time, trying to get a word in but finding it impossible, because Abram Markovitch was going strong and it would have been as much a pity to interrupt him as it would be a pity to waken a soundly sleeping person. Luckily for Masha, Tamara Shostepol arrived. And when Tamara arrived she politely sent Abram Markovitch from the room, asking him to tell Rosa she had a guest for tea.

"Not for tea," Masha corrected her, "but for a week or for two weeks, until I find a safe refuge. I hope you don't mind bringing in another bed?"

Tamara reddened. Itzikl Shostepol's daughter was not

sufficiently democratic to deal easily with a situation that came so naturally to the genuinely democratic Masha Bashevitch. Tamara told her she would be happy to have her stay not only two or three weeks but two or three months, the entire winter. And she soon changed the subject to the commune. How was it going there? How was Malkin? And she talked about Abram Markovitch, what a babbler he was but nevertheless a good person, a jewel, but a babbler, and about his wife, Rosa, who was a relative of hers.

"I'm not saying this just because she is a relative," said Tamara, "but when you get to know her better, you yourself will say that she is not just a woman but an angel! They have a child—that is to say, they have many children, but they have this one child, Zusya is his name, a four-year-old boy, and I can't imagine what he will grow up to be! Smart as a whip, good as an angel, and is he beautiful! Have you ever seen Raphael's self-portrait? Ah! I forgot that you are a . . . a . . . that you don't approve of art."

"You are greatly mistaken, Tamara. I love true art and little children too," said Masha, and Tamara responded with a sigh. She reminded herself that she, Tamara Shostepol, had been in Petersburg for quite a while and had still accomplished nothing, and she was envious of her friend Masha, deeply envious, but she didn't have the courage to say this. She opened the door, looked out and called, "Zusya! Nana! No one's here." And then she said to Masha, "Do you have any letters from home? Do they write?"

"Very often!" Masha answered her with a laugh. "Too often. Almost every day I get letters from my family, from my brothers, from my parents—especially from my father! He writes to me every other day and I have to write *him* every other day. And not just short letters but long megillahs full of details—what's happening and especially about the 'revolution.' He's become a revolutionary, a fanatic revolutionary!"

Masha burst out laughing, displaying her fine white healthy teeth that no dentist had ever had the opportunity to touch with his shiny instruments, and again Tamara was envious of her, because she was in such frequent touch with her family and because of her perfect white teeth.

"Here's the samovar!" announced the little barefooted shikseh Masha, the one with the large beads.

8

Masha Bashevitch at Tamara Shostepol's

It had been a long time since Masha had felt as good as she now felt sitting at the table of Tamara Shostepol's relatives. There she found an entire family, a nest, a coop alive with little chicks. The table was laid out with sliced bread and cheese, butter and jam. Next to the samovar sat Abram Markovitch's wife, Rosa, still a fresh-faced, lovely woman, surrounded by a flock of children, one smaller than the next. Each child was a world in himself—each with his own whims, his own ideas, his own tastes and inclinations. And the happy mother hen, Rosa, sat at the samovar checking what each one needed and what each one wanted, and in a moment it would appear. She was not troubled by their caprices. If they began to fight, she would separate them; if one started to cry, his tears would be dried; if a child laughed, his mother would laugh with him, beaming with pride, delight, and pleasure in her family.

Which of them did the mother love the most? It would be no contradiction for me to say she loved each child more than the next, as every child possessed something special another lacked. Still, there existed in this household a center, a focus around whom everything rotated as around a sun, whom all loved unstintingly without limit, who provided everyone with a reason for living, each person finding his own reason. That was Zusya!

Tamara Shostepol owned a large collection of photographs of this child. Abram Markovitch had many times wanted to paint a portrait of Zusya (Abram Markovitch was a bit of an artist), but the entire family, except for Rosa, refused to allow it, strongly protesting lest the father do injustice to Zusya's natural endowments. The father was both pleased and hurt—pleased because he was the father of this child and hurt because they didn't have confidence in his artistic ability. And so he decided instead to write a song about him, a lengthy song. But the song turned out even worse than the painting might have. No one liked the song except Rosa; she liked everything. Whatever Abram Markovitch said or wrote was good, was sweet, was beautiful. No one believed in Abram Markovitch's talents as much as his wife, Rosa. He himself didn't believe in them as much as Rosa did. To her, "Abrasha" was a genius whom no one understood or appreciated, because if everyone understood or appreciated him as much as she, he wouldn't have to waste so much precious time at the print shop, which barely provided them with a livelihood. If the world were a little more discriminating, Rosa thought, a publisher would have turned up a long time ago who would have published all the poems he had written since they were engaged. If the world were a little more discriminating, Rosa thought further, an interested buyer would have turned up who would have bought up all those paintings that he had been working on since she knew him. And Rosa glanced at the walls, which were hung with sketches and with paintings, the majority of them unfinished, and she remembered that in the attic there lay three times as many works of art, also unfinished.

And she remembered how many poems, songs, and unfinished novels lay in all the closets and in all the table drawers and even in the cupboards of the laundry room, where whole packets of manuscripts lay. God forbid if she dared even *think* of housecleaning, throwing out or burning anything! You may not believe it, but Rosa was familiar with all those immortal works. Rosa had read every poem, ballad, sketch, story, and novel. Well, she herself hadn't read them; her husband had read them to her, and not just once but many times. It was likely Rosa knew her husband's work even better than he, the creator himself, did. How often had Abram Markovitch asked Rosa the name of one or another hero from such and such a novel. "Tell me, was it Silverstein?" "No, my love," Rosa would answer, "you are mistaken."

To Abram Markovitch, Rosa's authoritative critique was the best, the wisest, and most sincere. One didn't dare show one's work to other critics; they undid one's best work, usually out of envy. They begrudged you your success! How could you compare a stranger to one's own wife? For instance, would a stranger sit down and praise a person, let him say what was in his heart, comfort him so that he wouldn't worry whether the world recognized him or not?

"Just wait, my love, a time will come when the world will recognize you too," Rosa consoled him. "Now they are busy with Tolstoy, with Gorky—they are creating sensations! Just wait till your first book of poems comes out—how are you doing with it? It isn't

80

finished yet? How many copies are you printing? Only two thousand? Ridiculous! Two hundred thousand at the very least!"

And both of them sat down to figure out how much they would make if they were, for example, to publish "The Collected Poems of Abram Markovitch." The figures were easy to calculate. The population of the country was 140 million. Let us say only one-tenth could read—so there would be 14 million buyers. How much would it cost to print a book? That Abram Markovitch knew well—he did have a print shop—but that meant nothing. The most important thing was the recognition, the reputation!

And the happy couple were carried away on the light wings of rich fantasy to the realm of imagination, to a Garden of Eden created by themselves. Meanwhile, in his own shop, Abram Markovitch had begun typesetting his early poems in a book entitled *The Young Harp,* which at first had encountered problems with the censor, who kept Abram busy writing and protesting for one and a half years, until God had pity on him and the censor approved it. *The Young Harp* came out in print, nicely illustrated with a harp and a hand playing it. But if one doesn't have luck, talent doesn't help! Tolstoy and Gorky and Chekhov and the others were selling in the hundreds of thousands, and *The Young Harp* by Abram Markovitch lay in the attic (of the 2000 copies printed, 1941 lay untouched). Well, wouldn't that be enough to shatter a man? Didn't Abram Markovitch have the right to rage and fume? But luckily he had such a wife as Rosa and such a precious jewel as Zusya.

"What do you think of our Zusya?" Abram said to their guest, Masha.

When she saw Zusya for the first time Masha almost ate him up alive. Not only was she enchanted by his white, marblelike, angelic little face, his long silken curls, deep sky-blue eyes, sculpted little nose, small mouth, perfect chin, classic composition of features, and extraordinary grace—he bewitched her with his comprehension, with his poise, with his talk and his vocabulary. He put such questions to her and answered her in such a clever, bright way that Masha was completely won over. She became deeply attached to the child, and her love for him grew day by day to the point that she once confessed to Tamara that she felt closer to this child than to her own little sisters and brothers, and that she could never imagine being separated from Zusya, who had so unexpectedly taken up such an important place in her life.

Whenever she had a free moment she spent it with Zusya—teaching Zusya, reading to Zusya, playing with Zusya. Enjoying Zusya was for Masha among the greatest pleasures in her life. When Masha came home Zusya was the first to greet her. When Masha woke up in the morning—there was Zusya. It was a delight for Masha to sit down and tell Zusya stories. Masha was a great storyteller, and Zusya adored stories more than anything else. Masha would sit down and tell him one story after another, and Zusya would open his perfectly shaped little lips and his sky-blue eyes and would gaze at Masha with complete understanding, like a truly knowing person, and, like a truly knowing person, he would laugh where it was appropriate to laugh and cry where one should cry.

Looking at this young creature, at this gifted child, so full of life, no one would have predicted that he would be the first victim of the impending storm. . . .

In the short time that Masha spent as Tamara Shostepol's guest she came to love Tamara as her own sister and became deeply attached to her. Masha didn't have to wait till her friend poured out her heart and soul to her. She knew Tamara's life, as it were, by heart. Tamara was taken aback when she found out Masha knew of her romance with the young Romanenko. That was on the day after Masha moved in with Tamara. She noticed on Tamara's desk a portrait in a small silver frame.

"Ah!" said Masha, glancing at the portrait. "That's Romanenko. He will be speaking tonight at the large racecourse. It's a shame I can't be there—I'm busy elsewhere. But he knows I can't come."

"You know each other?" Tamara said, and involuntarily her voice revealed a feeling of . . . jealousy? No! Romanenko was too sacred to her—Masha was above that! Then what was it?

Masha, however, quickly relieved her embarrassment. She told her, "You don't have to worry about it. I knew Romanenko long before you did. That he loves you is a fact. You worship him, and he deserves it, but I must tell you frankly—you know there can be no other way for me—you will never be happy, not you, not he. Do you want to know why? You forget he lives on a volcano, and you were born into another kind of life."

This was said so earnestly and in a tone so soft and gentle that Tamara could not feel insulted. She replied calmly, "You want to tell me I am no heroine, that I'm not worthy, that—"

"You are mistaken! That's not what I was saying to you!" Masha stopped her from going further. "I didn't mean to hurt your feelings. On the contrary, I love people like you. You are life itself and you were created for living. I would also want to be as you are. But I will never be that way. The times are at fault. We live in a bitter time, and circumstances have worked out for me so I don't know today where I will be tomorrow. The same is true for him, for Romanenko. I hope I'm wrong, but I see him far, far from here!"

"For me nothing is too far!" Tamara said passionately. "Where he is, that's where I'll be! There is no power on earth that will stop me or separate me from this man except death."

"Anyone else in your place would say the same. I think more highly of you for it," Masha said to her, "but I can't be silent and must tell you what I mean. I feel sorry for you, Tamara, but even more for your parents."

"My parents?" Tamara's eyes blazed. "Do we live for our parents? Why don't you feel sorry for your parents?"

"How do you know I don't?"

At that point Abram Markovitch came along and their talk was interrupted.

9

They Are Arrested!

In Abram Markovitch's house all its residents, from
Abram Markovitch himself to the little shikseh with the
large beads to the very youngest, Zusya, were deep in
that sweet slumber visited by the gentle angel who
weaves sweet dreams. Ah, dreams! Everyone finds in
his dreams what he desires, what he seeks. For instance,
Abram Markovitch delighted in images of his books
and paintings by the thousands, by the millions! People
were beating his door down! They all wanted his book
of poems, *The Young Harp*—he couldn't pack the vol-
umes fast enough and had to send many customers to
Rosa. And Rosa had an even better dream: a mass of
people, a procession, and right in its midst marched
Abram and all the children, with Zusya in front carrying his father's *The Young Harp*. The crowd was thun-
dering, shouting, "Long live the immortal creator of the
immortal *Harp!*" Behind him, with bowed heads, came

Count Tolstoy, Maxim Gorky, Anton Chekhov, Goethe, Schiller, Shakespeare, Mark Twain, and other famous writers, and all were weeping. In *her* dream Tamara Shostepol saw Romanenko holding a sign with large letters, CONSTITUTION! And Masha Bashevitch, sleeping in her cot beside Tamara's bed, dreamed of a parliament. She saw herself standing alone in the parliament on the speaker's platform, her hands at her sides. The walls were hung with proclamations, LONG LIVE FREEDOM! Masha, the little shikseh with the large beads, dreamed of red, green, blue, white, and yellow beads. Zusya's nana dreamed she was sitting on a long bench in a kindergarten with many other nanas, chatting. And Zusya himself saw before him bicycles and clocks, clocks and bicycles—rolling, spinning, turning, flying, flying!

Suddenly—Crash! Crash! Bang-bang! Bang-bang! Bang-bang! The windows shook, the door burst open. In a moment the house was filled with police. Everyone woke up, frightened to death, their teeth chattering with fear. The old nana crossed herself, prayed to God for help. Even little Zusya, who had just seen so many bicycles and so many clocks, sat up in his bed, opened his large, deep, sky-blue eyes, and asked the nana in a whisper, "Nana, is there a fire?"

"No, child, there's no fire, there's no fire. God is with us!"

"What, then? Robbers?" Zusya asked and threw off his covers, trying to climb out of bed.

"No, child, not robbers!" the nana answered and covered him up again. "Who ever heard of such nonsense!"

"Then what's happening?"

"Police!" the old nana said, crossing herself and invoking Jesus' name.

"But why at night?" Zusya kept asking one question

after another, not minding the old nana, who wanted him to lie down. Zusya wanted to see what kind of police these were, what they were doing there, and why at night? And Zusya saw that policemen with shiny epaulettes and gold buttons were opening all the drawers and all the cupboards and all the chests, leafing through books, packing away papers, and taking his father's books. His father stood trembling and his mother was wiping his forehead. And there was Auntie Tamara standing next to Auntie Masha, who was looking at her as if Auntie Tamara were about to die. . . . And Masha was already dressed, her hat perched on her bobbed hair, her hands at her sides, talking to a handsome officer with black muttonchop sideburns, and off to the side stood a dark-haired young man in an olive-colored overcoat, rubbing his hands together.

And Auntie Masha went over to Zusya, embraced him and drew him to herself tightly, kissed his eyes, his forehead, and his head, and it seemed to him her hands were cold and her eyes moist, and she said to him with a smile, "Zusya! You won't forget your Auntie Masha?"

And Zusya threw his arms around Masha's white neck and kissed her once, twice, ten times, twenty times, again and again and one last time, and then a sharp, steely voice was heard.

"Ready!" one of the officers said.

And they all stood up and they all were ready and they all left, all the officers with the shiny epaulettes and both aunties left. Little Masha with the large beads lit the way for them, and Zusya's father remained seated, shaking like a leaf, and his mother held him in her arms and wept, and all the children stood there, shivering and yawning, wanting to go back to sleep. And only Auntie Tamara and Auntie Masha were gone, and the old nana crossed herself, praying to Jesus. And little Zusya threw himself on his little white pillow and wept and wept and wept as only a four-year-old child, intelligent and sensitive beyond his years, can weep.

It was almost dawn and Abram Markovitch was still unable to calm himself, no matter what Rosa did to soothe him, rubbing his temples, using up all the eau de cologne. It was impossible for him to believe he was still a free man, and he kept asking his wife, Rosa, "Rosa, am I free?"

"You're free, Abrasha, you have always *been* free and you always *will* be free, always and forever!"

Abrasha was like a fragile child, like a pampered, overindulged only son to her. He always managed to get his way with her. Nothing was too difficult for her so long as Abrasha was happy. The best, the finest, and the first in the house was given to him, always to him, and Abrasha accepted it all, like a person who feels he is entitled to it. And should things not come as quickly as he wished or preferred or needed, he would become impatient, lose his temper, and vent his rage—on whom? Well, as always, on Rosa. And Rosa tolerated all of it out of love, convinced he was right. Tamara found it hard to stand by and witness his behavior. As a relative of Rosa's, she attempted several times to confront him, but Rosa stood up for her husband and defended him like the best lawyer. In the short time that Masha was Tamara's guest she also tried to come to Rosa's aid, and both girls set upon Abram Markovitch, calling him "satrap, despot," and other such names, making his life miserable, advancing astute arguments, until finally he became their sworn enemy, going around all puffed up like a turkey, and let out his bitter heart—at whom? Well, as always, at Rosa! And Rosa, as always accepting all of it out of love, would weep silently, wipe her eyes—and, never mind, was again the same lovely, fresh-faced, blooming Rosa, surrounded by her brood of little egoists, one more so than the next!

Nevertheless, when they took Masha and Tamara away, even such an egoist as Abram Markovitch was terrified for his life. For days afterward he paced about the house like a madman, raging (to Rosa) at the police, talking (to Rosa) against the government, calling it every vile name, and saying (to Rosa) that he himself would go to the prosecuting attorney, to the minister. What did he have to be afraid of? He was an innocent man, there was nothing in his books or writings.

"Nothing, Abrasha, nothing!" Rosa repeated, but Abram was displeased with this and took the other side.

"What do you mean, nothing? I have enough material in my poems, only disguised. Hah, Rosa?"

"Certainly, disguised!" Rosa went along, and it was left that no later than the following morning Abram Markovitch would go to see whether there wasn't something he could do to help the arrested girls. And that morning passed and another and two more mornings, and Abram Markovitch continued to seethe, boiling over with rage.

But it was all talk. Luckily, except for Rosa, no other human being heard him. Meanwhile Masha Bashevitch and Tamara Shostepol sat in prison, and Abram Markovitch did nothing on their behalf.

10

Sunday

From Saturday night on, soldiers began arriving. Entire squadrons took up positions on the outskirts of town, waiting. Thousands of workers put on their holiday attire, took their wives and children, and armed themselves with holy pictures and icons. Cossacks on horseback were galloping through the main streets of the city. The bridges over the Neva were thick with Cossacks, uhlans, and dragoons. Even the city fortress had been purposefully prepared.

At exactly nine o'clock in the morning small streams of people began flowing from the working-class neighborhoods, carrying their holy pictures, Father Gapon in the center of the gathered throng in his priestly garb, clasping a petition in his hand. Looking at this peaceful procession of men, women, and children, one would think this was some sacred patriotic holiday.

There is a saying, "A happy holiday, a happy year."

But this time it didn't hold true. The "happy holiday" was peaceful and pleasant; the "happy year" turned out to be vicious, frightful, evil, and bloody.

In honor of Sunday, Abram Markovitch's old nana dressed Zusya in his best holiday clothes à la Russe, which gave him a special charm, and, as she did every day, went for a stroll with the child. When she saw people walking on both sides of the street the old nana joined the crowd and followed along with them. The farther they went, the larger the stream of people grew, till it swelled into a sea whose waves swept people up and carried them, one wave after another, farther and farther. By the time the old nana decided to turn back, it had become impossible to do so. She and the child were carried forward against her will along with all the others. To her question, "Where is everyone going?" she received an answer from a worker who was dressed in Sunday clothes, also carrying a child of six in his arms. "We're going to petition."

"But why are there so many soldiers?" the nana asked further.

"In our honor, old woman, in our honor!"

No sooner had the worker replied than he was swept away by a wave of people, and that wave merged with a third wave of bodies. And the old nana gripped Zusya with her left hand as she crossed herself with her right, invoking Jesus' name. Her heart told her she had strayed into a bad situation, very bad. The nana paused at the bridge with the child and lifted him in her arms. She saw the holy pictures being carried aloft and the priest, Father Gapon, dressed in his robes and she heard the chanting of hymns.

"What's happening, nana?" Zusya asked her, looking right into the sea of people with his deep blue eyes.

"They are going to petition the Czar, my child."

But Zusya suddenly heard shooting. He asked the nana what did that mean, why were they shooting? The old woman explained that it was a custom to shoot when it was a holiday. Zusya looked intently with his deep blue eyes and saw people lying down and asked his nana what did that mean, why were people lying down? The old woman answered him that it was a custom for people to kneel down when they petitioned the Czar. And Zusya looked with his deep blue eyes and saw people falling, falling. He asked the nana what did that mean, why were people falling? And before the old woman could answer she felt a blow from behind, another from in front, and a shoving and crowding from all sides. And she saw people running, pushing, leaping over one another, and she heard strange sounds, the sounds of crying, screaming, shrieking, howling, wailing, and moaning. And the old woman crossed herself and muttered Jesus' name. And the same power, the same tide that had carried her this far was now carrying her back. She clasped the child to her heart, and Zusya held on tightly to the nana's neck, looking back into the crowd, and didn't stop asking questions. "Why are they running? Why are they shouting? Why are they shoving? Why are they crying?" And the old woman couldn't answer any of his questions. She felt that the multitude, not her own legs, was carrying her, and where she did not know. And now, suddenly plunging into the tide of people were huge, husky, broad-rumped horses, trampling the people. Soldiers with frightening faces and bared swords sat astride these huge, husky horses and were firing into the mass of humanity. People were dropping, dropping. And the old nana heard a loud crack and a strange cry issued from Zusya's throat. He let go of her neck and his little head slid down, down. And she felt a warm liquid on her neck and she saw blood running down her hand and she still didn't know whose blood it was, and she couldn't see that Zusya's head was shattered, broken, and she became faint and fell down with the dead child on the white, cold snow that was stained with red innocent blood. . . .

Thus began the Sunday known in Russian history as "Bloody Sunday."

11

Tamara Released

At first her arrest was for Tamara a source of gratification, one could even say pleasure and pride, for now that she was sitting in prison she could feel the equal of Masha and the other political prisoners. She was more concerned about what others might say of her being in prison than she was upset about having to be there a while. It was a time of conflict, the atmosphere was charged with strife, and it amounted to a disgrace for a girl to be in Petersburg with nothing more to do than study. But the longer she was confined in jail, the more uneasy she became, because she didn't know exactly why she had been arrested. She tried to guess, going over in her mind what meetings she might have attended. And she *had* attended many meetings. That past winter hardly a day had gone by without some meeting. Her only fear was that she might have been arrested on account of her relationship with Romanenko, and where he was now or what he was doing no one knew.

Finally she was taken from her cell and interrogated about what she knew of Miriam Gitl Bashevitch. Tamara answered that all she could say of Masha Bashevitch was that they came from the same city, had graduated from the same Gymnasium, and had recently shared a room—more than that she knew nothing. She was questioned repeatedly thereafter, always about Miriam Gitl Bashevitch, and finally they released her.

Like someone waking from a long sleep or illness, so Tamara felt once she was breathing the free air under the free sky, liberated from the heavy, suffocating prison atmosphere. New world! New sky! New skin! She was free, free, free!

Tamara Shostepol stepped into the first droshky she saw going by. The residential district looked like a battlefield that had been abandoned by the enemy as it moved on. On the Moyke, on Yekaterinski Canal, and here and there on the Nevki Prospect one could see an occasional patrol or a Cossack on foot or on horseback. It was already late in the day, yet Petersburg seemed steeped in darkness and cloaked in sorrow. Tamara had learned while in prison that something was happening in the city, but she couldn't figure out exactly what. She could see through her single small window how groups of students and workers were being brought in. She concluded that an extraordinary demonstration must have taken place and she deeply regretted not having participated in the event. But now she realized that around her were signs of a battle, and she asked the driver, a mere boy of seventeen or eighteen, wearing an oversized hat that kept falling down over his eyes, requiring him to shove it back constantly, "What happened here?"

"Nothing happened, miss," he replied in a high-pitched, childish voice, pushing his oversized cap back.

"They just shot up a few of our brothers. Broke a few bones," he added with a smile.

"Why?"

"How should I know? They say because people wanted to petition the Czar."

"So?"

"So they didn't let them."

"So?"

"So they set dragoons and Cossacks on them."

"So?"

"So they started to knock them down and knock them down and knock them down!"

The driver demonstrated with his hand how they knocked them down.

"Were many killed?" Tamara asked him.

"Plenty!" answered the driver, pushing his cap back.

"How many?" Tamara asked. 'Ten people? Twenty? Fifty? A hundred?"

"Go higher!" he said in his high-pitched voice.

"Two hundred? Five hundred?"

"Higher!"

"A thousand?"

"Higher!"

"Two thousand?"

"Still higher!"

Tamara suspected she was dealing with someone who couldn't count past ten. She stopped talking to him, arrived at her residence, paid the driver, and rang the doorbell. The little shikseh with the large beads came to the door. Her eyes were red and swollen and she was without her usual little laugh.

"What's happened?" Tamara questioned her anxiously.

"Our little boy!" The little shikseh tried to answer and couldn't speak any further.

And when Tamara entered and found Abram Markovitch, Rosa, and all the children sitting on the floor in their stockinged feet, their faces gray as ash and without expression, she realized what had happened. They told her everything, everything.

Later she was to discover that Romanenko had disappeared; no one knew where he was. Some said he had been arrested, others said sent into exile.

12

On Grief and Sorrow

Forlorn, preoccupied, and aimless, a worried Tamara Shostepol wandered the streets of Petersburg, her thoughts full of all the events she had lived through in that great turbulent city of Petersburg from the time she had arrived until that very day: all that had happened, all the images, all her encounters, all the people—Zusya, Rosa, Masha. But one person had entirely left her thoughts, as if he had never existed at all. And yet that person had thought about Tamara, one could say, more than anyone else. That person was the student, Sasha Safranovitch—and he was now approaching her with a friendly smile on his lips and with rosy cheeks that, it almost seemed, were trying to compete with the red hair on his head and the red beard he had recently acquired.

It was obvious from Sasha's face how happy and lucky he felt himself to be to have come across the very one he had been seeking, yearning for, desiring.

"One can never find you at home!" Sasha said to her, and for once Tamara was happy to meet Sasha. And like a good friend, she brought him up-to-date on everything that had happened—the story of Masha Bashevitch's imprisonment, the story of her own arrest in all its smallest details, concluding with all the events and circumstances surrounding the terrible tragedy of little Zusya. She told him that she couldn't bear to witness his mother's grief. Every day living there was an agony.

But that wasn't the entire truth, that was not the real reason for her sadness. For the real reason one had to search somewhere else, deeper. Sasha Safranovitch talked to her sympathetically and consoled her, telling her there had to be sacrifices. Without sacrifices no ideal could be attained. He provided her with a thousand examples from Jewish history and gave her an entire lecture on ancient Jewish history, ending with these words: "The ideals of fairness, freedom, equality, and justice are our highest aspirations, so that even in their prayers Jews try to persuade God to rule the universe with fairness and justice. What kind of divine justice would it be if all men weren't equal?"

Sasha Safranovitch's words were to Fraulein Shostepol soothing and healing. It seemed to him that she had never listened to him before with such interest as on that day. Actually, Tamara was listening to him less intently than ever; her thoughts were far removed. She was listening to this student, this fanatic Jewish nationalist, but more important, she envied him as she envied her friend Masha Bashevitch, because they were doers and she, Tamara, was not.

During the entire time these young people found themselves in Petersburg they had rarely seen each other, and when they had talked, it was for no more than half an hour or so. But each time Safranovitch had returned to his theme: Judaism, Jewish history, the Jewish language. Mainly he reprimanded Tamara for not learning to speak Yiddish. "Why do we all study other foreign languages," he kept complaining to her, "but we are ashamed of our own language?" Tamara would usually answer just enough to be rid of him. "Where could I study Yiddish here in Petersburg? Who would want to undertake to teach it?" "Just say the word," Sasha would answer, "just say the word that you want to learn the language and a teacher will be found for you."

It was apparent he was speaking of himself. But Tamara was always busy; there was no time. Too many obligations. "Not Jewish obligations," Safranovitch would say and would quote a verse from the Song of Songs: "They made me the keeper of the vineyards; but mine own vineyard have I not kept." He would repeat the verse several times until she had learned it by heart.

Tamara loved to tease the redheaded student, the fanatic nationalist. She would say to him with a laugh, "What did you once say? 'They made me the keeper of the vineyards, but mine own vineyard have I not kept'?"

"*I* didn't say it," Safranovitch answered her, "King Solomon once said it in his Song of Songs. Ach, Fraulein Shostepol! It's high time you knew more of your own literary accomplishments. If you like, I will show you something you will enjoy. It's a poem, a bloody poem, a pogrom poem by . . . by a very famous Jewish poet. I'll read it to you in our own ancient, melodious language and then translate it for you so you can understand it."

And Sasha Safranovitch didn't wait to be urged but removed from his breast pocket several pages that had been torn out of a book and read aloud in a clear voice the powerful lines of the very powerful poem that had (in Safranovitch's opinion) no equal in world poetry, in the melodious language that had (in Safranovitch's opinion) no equal in world literature! He spat out the words with great passion, translating every word for Tamara as he went along, gesticulating to further clarify the meaning, attracting more than a few passersby, who stopped to watch the couple on the sidewalk.

> . . . Of steel and iron, cold and hard and dumb,
> Forge for yourself a heart, O man, and come!
> Come to the city of slaughter,
> See with your own eyes,
> Feel with your own hands,
> On fences, posts and gates,
> On flagstones, walls, and window grates,
> The dry, darkening blood and brains
> From a brother's throat and head.
> Wander through the widespread ruins,
> Through shattered walls and twisted doors,
> By windswept hearths and chimneys bled
> Of their human warmth,
> By bare blackened stones, half-charred bricks
> On which fire, blade and axe
> Played a wild tattoo. . . .

Tamara Shostepol listened intently to the words. Her large lovely dark eyes became serious. And Sasha turned a page of the poem and read further in the same manner and with even more passion:

> . . . Running off? Take to your heels!
> Hide in the innocent fields.
> Safe a while!
> Near you a manure pile
> Where two lie slain: a Jew and his dog.

The day before both beheaded by one stroke of
  an axe.
Today dragged through mire on their blood-
  soaked backs
By a swine snorting and snuffling in their
  mingled blood.
Wait, tomorrow a fresh rain will come
To rinse the blood away so it won't cry out
From its midden heap to heaven, "Help!"
Or has it already sunk into the abyss
Perhaps to nurse a twisted hedge of thorns.
And tomorrow—as today, as yesterday—the
  sun,
Its warmth not lessened in the least,
Will softly, silently, rise up in the east.

And Tamara's large lovely dark eyes became even
larger and more lovely and she was reminded of that
Bloody Sunday in Petersburg, which she herself had not
experienced but had heard about from others, and she
said to him, "What is his name, your poet?"

"*My* poet," Safranovitch answered her with a little
smile, "is called Bialik, Chaim Nachman Bialik."

"This Bialik is quite a poet! Go on, read some more."

There was certainly no need to urge Sasha Safranovitch to go on reading Bialik! Sasha obliged her,
turned a page of the poem, and read further:

Don't lift your head—there's no heaven!
Only a roof, an empty roof, covered with
  blackened shingles.
There a spider hangs—go ask him.
He saw everything, he witnessed everything.
A surviving witness on the ceiling.
Let him tell you about all he saw:

About a belly stuffed with feathers,
About little noses split by nails, heads broken
   by hammers,
About slaughtered people, heads down, like
   geese,
Hanging from the balcony under the roof.
About a child still asleep, its mother's breast,
Crushed and lifeless, filling its mouth.
And about another child torn in two
While still alive, its last scream also torn in two,
Uttering, "Ma—!

And Tamara was reminded of Zusya's death as told
her by the old nana, and her eyes filled with tears. And
Sasha turned another page of the bloody poem and read
on:

Crawl on, O man, crawl further. I will show
   you
Wonders in pigsties
Where hidden in the offal your own eyes
Will behold your brothers—the heirs of the
   Hasmoneans,
Descendents of the eternally holy ones.
In every hole you will find three minyans
Which took refuge there on that day of
   slaughter . . .
Now go where the green field begins
At whose edge there is a stable in ruins
Where shattered wheels lie strewn about
Bespattered with blood and innards,
Their spokes sprung loose from the rim
   reaching out
Like murderous fingers for someone's throat.
Be patient, at evening when the sun,

Fiery and blood-red, sets in the west,
Steal quietly into the ruined stable
And prepare to vanish in a gulf of terror . . .

"So, is there not a single ray of light in the rest of this poem? No shred of hope for tomorrow?" Tamara Shostepol said to Sasha Safranovitch. Instead of answering her he turned several pages of the poem and read more:

And tomorrow, son of Adam, go out into the
     square,
Behold a market, a market of human bric-a-
     brac!
Dejected, barely moving human insects,
Their bodies twisted and fractured,
Wrapped in rags, all skin and bones,
Dazed children crawling on crippled limbs,
Young women like crones
Bent over, thin, dried out, their faces slack.
Like locusts, the plague of summer's end,
They assault door and portal, drum on window
     panes,
Besiege the thresholds front and back,
Stretch out crooked hands used to the beggar's
     game,
Exposing running sores and wounds in bold
Excess, rolling tormented eyes heavenward,
Like slaves, like a beaten dog before its master,
A groschen for a wound! A groschen for a
     wound!
A groschen for a violated daughter! . . .

"So this is the consolation? A fine perspective! A shining future for a people!" said Tamara, and Sasha read further:

Drag yourselves to the graveyards with your
    empty sacks,
Dig up the white bones
Of your holy dead from their graves,
Fill up the sacks, each one his own,
And set forth with backs bent,
Journeying from town to town, from fair to
    fair,
And under the strangers' high windows
Sing out the beggar's hoarse lament—

"Is there no hope at all for the future, ever? Not even
a tiny glimmer of vengeance?" Tamara said, her large
lovely eyes flashing, and Sasha, instead of answering
her, turned a page of Bialik's mighty poem and read on:

. . . His heart became as a barren desert,
No seed of vengeance, not a single blade of
    hatred.
Do you hear? They beat their hollow chests—
    Ashamnu!
They pray to me to forgive their sins.
Does a shadow on the wall sin?
Does a shattered skull sin? A trampled worm
    sin?
What are they praying for?
Why do they stretch out their hands to me?
Where are their fists? Where is their thunder
That should settle the score
For all the generations,
Destroy the world, tear down the heavens,
Overturn my glorious throne?! . . .

"Ah? *Those* are words!" cried Tamara with enthusiasm. "Your Bialik is a poet! A great poet!"

"*My* Bialik is also *your* Bialik!" said Safranovitch to her, and they fell into a discussion about the Jewish people and about their prospects and about their prophets and about the Messiah.

"Do you also believe in the Messiah?" Tamara asked him.

"Of course!" Sasha replied and was happy to have a subject to discuss with Tamara. And he explained what his understanding was of the Messiah and why the Messiah could not come. He wanted to convince her that at that particular time in history, when there existed so many schisms among the people, the Messiah could not come. The Messiah could come only when all the people wanted to hear him and all wanted to understand him. Moses, for example, would never have succeeded with today's Jews, because there was no unified Jewish people that could appreciate that only in unity was there strength.

And Sasha was pleased with himself and with his splendid speech, certain that he was making a better impression on Tamara than ever. He felt certain she had heard him and that he had had an effect on her. He sensed that she had warmed toward him. He was oblivious of the fact that from the Neva a wind had started up that made his face smart, stung his nose, and chilled him to the bone. He did not realize that both of them were standing at the door of Tamara's rooms, and he became fully aware of it only when Tamara rang the doorbell.

"Come inside, you are frozen!" Tamara said to him and bestowed upon him a look from her lovely dark eyes, and he imagined that Tamara had never looked at him this way before. . . .

It was already late when Sasha made his way home by sleigh over the crunchy, gleaming snow through the brightly lit streets of Petersburg. From the Neva a cold snow-laden wind was blowing that was more vexing than the stinging frost to which people had become accustomed. Sasha's red face turned blue and his ears burned. His nose also suffered from the cold, and no amount of rubbing or covering up or wrapping himself in the soft lambskin collar of his warm winter overcoat helped. But what did that matter to this lucky man compared to the warm benevolent look from Tamara's large lovely dark eyes, which was enough to blunt the sharpest wind, to thaw the greatest frost? Sasha went over every word Tamara had said that day, remembered her every movement, her every glance, and he imagined—or so he wanted to believe—that Tamara had never been so kind to him, so friendly, so responsive and close as on that day, and he came away from her with more hope than ever before!

PART TWO

1

Fathers and Children

At the very beginning of our novel, in the first chapter, we left Itzikl Shostepol, his wife, Shivka, and Solomon Safranovitch awaiting their children, Tamara and Sasha, who were coming home for Pesach.

"Why don't you go down to the railroad station?" Shivka urged her husband, glancing at the clock.

"What an idea! What difference will that make? Will that make her come home any sooner?" answered her husband sarcastically, as a man will when he is not happy. But shortly after, when the same thought occurred to him, he decided it would, in fact, be a good idea to go down to the train station. What could he lose? And he put on his overcoat, took his umbrella, and prepared to leave.

"Where are you going?" Shivka asked him.

"Nowhere," her husband answered. "I thought I would drive down to the station to see why the train is so late."

"I just said the very same thing!"

"So? You said it, so what? What difference does that make?"

And Itzikl Shostepol departed, hailed a droshky outside the house, and sped off to the train station.

The pharmacist Safranovitch had arrived at the same decision, but he had no wife to consult, as he had been a widower for fifteen years. Our pharmacist, as he said of himself, was not one of those men who rush off to marry a second time. First of all, he didn't have the time, and second of all, there was no one in town who suited him, and third of all, why should she inherit the pharmacy?

When Itzikl Shostepol arrived at the train station he found the pharmacist already pacing up and down, cane in hand, wearing his blue-tinted spectacles, but Itzikl pretended not to notice him. Instead he began to set his pocket watch by the large station clock. The pharmacist was, in fact, doing the same: he also had removed his gold watch from his pocket and was standing in front of the station clock peering through his blue-tinted spectacles, first at the clock, then at his watch, noticing that his gold watch was running almost one and a half minutes fast. And Shostepol was noting that *his* watch was running almost five minutes slow. Those few minutes' difference provoked an unexpected conversation between our two neighbors which we relate word for word, although we cannot say which of the two started to speak first.

"I can't believe my watch is off."

"Mine is off too."

"Surprisingly, my watch is correct by the town clock."

"Apparently the *Poyezer* is late."

"How come an express train is late?"

"It happens. Are you waiting for someone?"

"And you?"

And both fathers put their watches back in their pockets, parted, one this way and one that, having run out of conversation.

Bear in mind that that's an expression people use. Had they wanted to, had they not been so proud and stubborn, they would have had much to talk about. Each one could have gone on and on. Each had a heart charged with pain that begged to be expressed, to be poured out, but each man felt it beneath his dignity to do so before the other.

What do I have in common with that ordinary pharmacist? thought Shostepol, swinging his umbrella.

I detest that phony pious "Yiddash," with his umbrella and his black eyes that look right into your soul! thought Safranovitch the pharmacist, and both of them paced up and down the wide platform, one this way and one that, each one deep in his own thoughts, each with his own burden.

And what, one might ask, could Itzikl Shostepol's burden be when his business affairs were, thank God, prospering? That past winter he had concluded a lucrative prison deal. I mean, he wasn't, God forbid, in prison; rather, he provided the food for the prisoners, and was lucky enough to have a cooperative warden, one who accepted a little something on the side. Recently he had sold lumber to the barracks, which also involved getting around a subcontractor. But then there were all those "takers." The top man "took," the bottom man "took," the captain "took," the commander "took," the adjutant "took," and the general "took." Let them all "take" the plague, because not only did they take your money, they took your health away as well.

Recently he had been involved in several lawsuits over his business dealings. Itzikl Shostepol, you should know, was a man who loved litigation. At the very same time he was making a business deal he was already working it out so that he could sue later. When he was negotiating a contract he would insist on adding so many clauses and codicils that ten lawyers couldn't disentangle them. A lawyer once asked him, "Pani Shostepol, instead of writing the contract yourself and then coming to me to rescue you, why don't you go to a lawyer first and let him write it, so you can be saved the trouble of having to sue afterward?" Shostepol replied to this suggestion in all seriousness, "It costs money to have a lawyer write a contract." "And suing doesn't cost money?" "What can I do? I have to protect my money!"

That was Itzikl Shostepol's reply and that's how he "protected" his money—that is, it cost him three times as much and he frequently lost thousands, almost went bankrupt, carried on lawsuits lasting years, and wore himself out to win a case. And *that* was the triumph he lived for! Vengeance and success—important things! For the sake of success Itzikl Shostepol would wade up to his neck in blood! The possibility that he might lose was never considered. Itzikl could boast that no one had ever bested him. The only one who could make that claim was Tamara. But what could one do? A daughter, an only child—and a gifted one into the bargain—a daughter he loved with all his heart and soul. He would literally die for her! How many times had he suddenly awakened from a deep sleep before dawn in a state of agitation and ordered his bags packed.

"Where are you going?" Shivka would ask him.

"To Petersburg! Why is she living there? Why all this studying? What good are all these courses? Why this medicine? Why become a doctor? Who ever heard of female doctors? That's all we need!"

Itzikl would work himself up to such a state that he would sit himself down to write Tamara a letter, one she would never forget, full of reprimands. But no sooner would he take pen in hand and set down the first words, "Dear daughter," than his rage would subside and he would write instead how much he missed her and how she should, in the name of God, write that she was well and be sure to ask if she needed money or anything else. He became sweet as honey, gentle as a lamb, and his heart was full of loving feelings. What a strange father this Itzikl Shostepol was!

Yes, a strange father. It exasperated him greatly that he, Itzikl Shostepol, had to wait for his child on the same platform with the pharmacist, whose own child was surely coming from the same city as his daughter and was surely sitting and talking with her in one compartment. What could they be talking about? Perhaps they already knew each other so well they were talking of marriage? Could one put it past modern children? And he broke out in a cold sweat at the very thought. He began pacing faster, swinging his umbrella even harder, thinking, Why did I deserve such a daughter?

That very question Itzikl Shostepol was asking about his daughter, Solomon Safranovitch was asking about his son.

The pharmacist's business was also doing well. He had paid off the pharmacy long ago and was able to put some savings in the bank. He was thinking of buying a small house of his own, not too far away, also on that same Vasilchikover Street. The house belonged to a gentile spinster who visited his pharmacy almost every day with a big dog named Hector. She would buy some foolish item for five groschen and would talk on for half an hour and sometimes more. She tried to persuade him to buy her house, which had a garden, a very lovely garden. Where could he find a garden with such grapes and with such pears, as well as a good cellar and a fine stable, as hers?

Solomon Safranovitch loved Sasha, admired and idealized him, but understood him not at all. He would write his son informative letters and would receive frequent letters in return—fine letters but strange beyond comprehension. Safranovitch simply did not understand his son. For the longest time he had been trying to find out from him what made him so devoted to Yiddishkeit. What was it? Was it a religious conviction? Or had he become orthodox? If so, was that no more than a crazy idea? (He didn't want to call it a meshugas.) Sasha quieted his father's fears on this score by telling him it had nothing to do with religion but with nationalistic feeling, with love for a people, with deeply felt, pure patriotism.

The world was topsy-turvy! Solomon Safranovitch had struggled so hard for his own education, living in the attic of his miserable, fanatically pious parents' hovel, studying Latin, running away from home barefooted, starving, and eventually passing the pharmacy examinations, barely surviving to see the day when he became an apprentice. He had had to crawl on his hands and knees before he was even *allowed* to take the examinations, and now that, with God's help, he had become a pharmacist with a good name and a large clientele, especially among gentiles (he avoided Jews), he, Safranovitch, had to raise a son who wrote him letters containing these sentiments: "Dear Father, You must realize the times are changing. The need to grovel before the gentile landowner is over! The habit of crawling on one's hands and knees before everything that is not Jewish is now out of style."

In another letter Sasha wrote: "Dear Father, If we really want to win the sympathy of the Russian people we don't need to prove to them that we are either better or worse than they; we need only to show them we are *as good as they*. Then I am certain that the struggle our people are carrying on will prove successful and we will no longer need to rely on pity or favors."

And in a third letter Sasha wrote: "Dear Father, It is indeed a shame that I cannot write to you in Yiddish. You know very well how much I love the Russian language and Russian literature. But why shouldn't we use our own national language if we have one? Why should two Germans, Frenchmen, or Poles be able to converse with one another when they meet in America or anywhere in the world, and we cannot? We, who are more immigrants than all the immigrants in the world, we, who have been emigrating since the days of Abraham, need our national tongue more than any other people! Just imagine, dear Father, if I had grown up from childhood in another country and would now come home, do you realize that both of us, father and son, would not be able to converse? I took the liberty of asking my German and Polish friends in which language they wrote to their parents and they laughed at me and replied with a question, 'You're a Jew, so how do you write to your father, do you not write in Yiddish?' You can understand, dear Father, that I turned even redder than I am."

The pharmacist could not understand how he had raised such a son. He blamed himself for remaining a widower for fifteen years. Sasha had grown up without a mother, had likely come into contact with questionable friends in the Gymnasium. He recalled how Sasha was always being visited by poverty-stricken students, shabby boys who had previously studied in Talmud Torahs, among them either the shokhet's—ritual slaughterer's—or the rabbi's son, named either Cutler or Kessler—he never could remember. He remembered only that the Gymnasium uniform suited Cutler (or was it Kessler?) as a nosegay suits a pig, because his hair was very curly, his shoulders stooped, his hat pushed back on his head, and he spoke with a speech defect, gargling, "Safkhanovitch, " "Khussian histokhy."

A shame and an embarrassment for the gentiles! the pharmacist would think, his face reddening from ear to ear. All of them, all those little Jews are so eager to study! All those poor trash are pushing themselves into the Gymnasium!

And our pharmacist was furious at those rag-picking "little Jews" who elbowed into the Gymnasium so eager to study. He forgot that he himself was once a "little Jew," was himself a poor man's son, was also once in the position of having to study Latin in an attic.

When our young heroes arrived, the reunion was not as it should have been. Something was missing. The fathers and their children should have been truly happy to see one another. Tamara Shostepol *did* throw her arms around her father's neck and *did* kiss him, and Sasha Safranovitch *did* embrace the pharmacist as a son should embrace a father, but genuine affection was somehow absent on both sides—that sense of joyous celebration, that spontaneous enthusiasm, that keen excitement that sets everyone and everything whirling before one's eyes, creating a happy confusion, overflowing one's heart so that one almost cries out for joy.

Both fathers contemplated their children. Itzikl Shostepol looked at his daughter, who was wearing a small inexpensive hat, black and without feathers, on her thick black wavy hair. Across her chest she was carrying a man's small traveling bag. Her large lovely dark eyes were now clouded over with a strange melancholic seriousness. She had grown up, grown up! And Itzikl thought, Is this my daughter?

Those were also the pharmacist's thoughts as he gazed through his blue-tinted spectacles at Sasha, marveling at how he had grown up, how handsome he had become. Amazing! Red hair, a small red goatee, a bent nose, a real Jewish nose! The pharmacist tried to take the yellow bag from him, but Sasha wouldn't let him—he could do it alone.

"Do you know our neighbor's daughter, Fraulein Shostepol?" Sasha said to his father, and introduced him to Tamara, who introduced Sasha to her father as she said to him, "This is the pharmacist's son. You know who his father is."

And the four stood around at loose ends, unsure of what to do next or who should take the lead. And all four said at once, "Nu? Shall we go?"

And all four answered, "Let's go." And none of the four knew exactly where to go. But when they emerged from the station, and as the porters were grabbing for their luggage and the drivers were shouting and the traffic police were ordering them about, a carriage drove up, and before they knew it all the luggage had been placed on top of the carriage. One carriage was all that was necessary. They lived at the same address—why should they throw away money?"

On the front seat of the carriage Itzikl Shostepol sat next to Solomon Safranovitch, and opposite them, on a small bench, sat their children, Tamara and Sasha. The carriage rocked back and forth over the stones recently laid bare by the melting snow and the wheels sprayed the not quite dry erev-Pesach mud. The blowing wind was a mild, warm erev-Pesach wind, and the air smelled of erev Pesach, that familiar smell of a holiday so beloved by every Jew for its historic meaning, for its spirit of liberation, and for its concurrence with the time of nature's renewal.

"The air already smells of Pesach," commented Itzikl Shostepol, unable to find anything else to say to his uneasy neighbor. "Things will soon be turning green," the pharmacist added, so as not to appear unpleasant.

"Long live the Jewish Pesach!" Sasha cried out enthusiastically.

"Long live spring!" Tamara corrected him.

"Long live the holiday of freedom!" Sasha added.

"Long live freedom itself!" Tamara corrected him again. And a lively argument broke out between the two children. The parents sat and listened to them admiringly, each according to his perception and each with a different feeling in his heart.

"What a clever world it's become!" said Itzikl Shostepol, half ironically, half proudly, looking down at the handle of his umbrella with a mischievous smile.

"A topsy-turvy world!" the pharmacist answered, looking out at the houses through his blue-tinted spectacles.

And the carriage with its four occupants soon arrived in front of No. 13 Vasilchikover Street.

To be a bearer of good news is a great mitzvah among Jews: it gives pleasure, doesn't hurt anyone, and doesn't cost a cent.

When the carriage bearing the four occupants drove up to No. 13 Vasilchikover Street, it was spotted by Zissel, Nehemiah the shoemaker's wife, who also lived at No. 13.

Understandably, the shoemaker's flat was down below, in the basement. And since the windows were on street level, the shoemaker and his family had the best opportunity of seeing at close range anyone who passed by, and much before the other residents in the house.

"Look who has just driven up, big as life!" Zissel called out, and flew outside, while Nehemiah and the two boys sat engrossed in their work, hammering nails into the new shoes that Shivka Shostepol had ordered in honor of Pesach. Both boys, Chaim and Benny, soon bent down almost to the floor to see out the window and into the carriage, from which Sasha sprang out, after him Tamara, and after Tamara both neighbors, the pharmacist with his cane and Itzikl Shostepol with his umbrella.

"We have guests!" said Chaim, and Benny added, "The Zionist, the socialist, the bourgeois, and the proletarian!"

"What does that mean?" their father asked, and both his sons explained that four representatives of four different ideologies had arrived, and between the father and his children there followed a discussion about Zionism, socialism, capitalism, and proletarianism. Nehemiah couldn't understand what kind of a proletarian Safranovitch was. To the shoemaker a proletarian was a poor man, and a poor man could be only one who didn't have anything for Pesach. The elder son, Chaim, explained that one could have something for Pesach and still be a proletarian.

"A proletarian is anyone who works for a wage for the comfort of the bourgeoisie, so that a storekeeper is the same as a shoemaker."

"They're exact opposite!" said the father, hammering a nail into the heel of a shoe, and as he said those words our old acquaintances arrived, the cheerful tailor, Yudel

Katanti, ready with a verse and with a curse while not yet across the threshold.

"May a plague befall our little Jews and our rabbis, I mean your ordinary ones. I just this minute left the rabbiner himself. They aren't handing out *Maos Chitim* —Pesach charity—as they're supposed to. The one who needs it isn't getting anything, and the one who has pull and who knows someone gets and gets, may they get the cholera! What can I tell you? I gave the rabbiner whatever came to my tongue. I said to that fine man, I said, 'We elected you,' I said, 'to be our rabbiner in the city, so you have to,' I said, 'take care of the poor,' I said, 'according to Rashi.' Then in Russian he said, 'If that's the case, what's in it for me?'"

Zissel, the shoemaker's wife, ran upstairs to the wealthy Shivka Shostepol to tell her the good news about her daughter's arrival, not because Zissel was such a good friend of Shivka's but simply because it was considered a mitzvah for one Jew to bring another good news.

"God love you and your guest, your daughter has arrived!" But she was too late (a poor person has no luck). The mitzvah had been snatched away by Chava, the old woman, who was now running down the stairs from Shivka's.

"She knows already! Don't bother!" And by the time the shoemaker's wife went down again, Tamara had already greeted her mother, and the mother was crying on the daughter's shoulder, crying very hard! She apparently wanted to pour out all the troubles she had endured since Tamara had gone away, to pour out her longing, her indignities, her humiliations in front of others, her loneliness, and her troubles with her husband, who always let his bitterness out on her. And we all know how a mother can cry!

Shivka Shostepol had not as yet looked her fill at her daughter, when Chaska, the kitchen maid, came in with the news: "The wood hauler is here—he wants to see Tamara."

"Just what we needed! Tell him to go to the devil!" said Shivka.

"Call him in!" Tamara said, and in came Lippa Bashevitch with his broom beard to receive regards from his daughter Masha. And Tamara greeted him in a most friendly manner, led him into another room, and sat down to chat with him about his daughter Masha. And Itzikl Shostepol and his wife, Shivka, remained standing outside, looking at each other wordlessly, and each one sighed a deep, deep sigh from the bottom of the heart.

2

At the Pesach Seder

Who is this regal personage, this king with great deep-set eyes, his lustrous beard elegantly curled, appareled in pure white robes, a pure white silken cap on his head and pure white silken slippers on his feet, enthroned at the head of the table, reclining on comfortable oversized pillows, so relaxed, so calm, so gracious and friendly to everyone? Can this be Itzikl Shostepol, the perpetually overwrought, distracted, distraught, preoccupied Itzikl Shostepol? Where has his restless face gone, his rushing, his hurrying, his business affairs with all their machinations and entanglements, lawsuits and payoffs, involving half the world?

Who is this splended queen seated proudly at his right hand, adorned with pearls and diamonds that flash and bedazzle like the sparkling wine in the glistening decanters, endowing her once beautiful face with such charm and pride that it is impossible to recognize the perpetually worried and beset Shivka Shostepol, whose honor and dignity are constantly diminished at the hands of her despotic husband?

And who is this radiant, stately, beautiful princess with the great black eyes and with the shining black wavy hair so perfectly set off by her white dress, which her mother had, with tears, managed to convince her to wear at least once for her sake and for the sake of the sacred holiday, and who had obeyed her, unable to abide her mother's tears?

This scene between mother and daughter had taken place after the blessing of the candles. The father was still in shul, the mother stood appareled in silk, pearls, and diamonds before six large, ornate silver candlesticks surrounding an antique seven-armed candelabrum, her hands raised to closed eyes, making the blessing over the candles and weeping silently, so silently and forlornly that only he alone, the Blessed One, could hear. Tamara sat at a side table in her black everyday dress reading a book or perhaps thinking.

After finishing the candle blessing the mother approached the daughter, nervously cracking her knuckles, and sat down at her side. She began talking to her, not reprimanding her but quietly pouring out her heart to her child, her only consolation in this world, conveying to her by hints and subtle gestures what it was she had to endure from her husband. She wasn't, God forbid, blaming him, nor was she complaining about him, may her child have no worse a life than she has had with her husband, but a man is no more than a man, and especially such an excitable, overwrought person as he was, who never had a moment to himself except on Shabbos and on yomtov, and who always let his heart out to her for any reason at all: because the samovar wasn't ready on time, because some lawsuit wasn't going his way, because his daughter was in Petersburg—for everything, she, the mother was to blame, and she accepted it all out of love, because most likely God had meant it to be so and one cannot go against God.

So Shivka lamented to her daughter, wiping her eyes, which refused to stop weeping. And Tamara wanted to tell her that it was not God but she herself who was to blame for permitting herself to be trodden upon. And the mother couldn't stop pouring out her heart to the daughter whom she so wanted to see happy, but didn't know how she could manage it. She would gladly have sacrificed herself for her, have given her all her jewelry, these pearls and diamonds, and her whole life if need be. For her daughter's sake, she, Shivka Shostepol, Itzikl Shostepol's wife, would have become a slave.

So the mother spoke, and Tamara's heart was softened and her soul was moved. She wanted to comfort her mother, but she didn't know how. She felt remote, cut off from her mother. The mother didn't stop lamenting her miserable lot, which she had not deserved at the hands of God. Here was her only child, the apple of her eye, who could not make so much as one sacrifice for her mother, to grant her one little favor, providing her mother at least some pleasure for a few hours at the most, not more. So she prevailed upon her daughter to put on a white dress, "for my sake and for the sake of the blessed holiday." And there was no happier mother in the world than Shivka Shostepol, the splendid queen who reigned that night! And when the father arrived from shul with a hearty "Goot yomtov!" and saw Tamara all dressed for the holiday, he became even more regal, and his fatherly heart was even more joyful, and he forgave her all the humiliations and all the worries and all the sleepless nights and all the troubles he had endured till that night.

"Who will ask me the Four Questions?" said Itzikl Shostepol teasingly to his daughter, and was answered, "You won't be able to answer the Four Questions I will ask."

"Good, we'll see!" replied the happy father as he prepared for the seder ritual, setting out Haggadahs for the participants, even for Chava, the old domestic, and for Chaska, the kitchen maid, who, according to the old Jewish custom, sat at the seder table together with the rest of the family, because at the Pesach seder all are equal—there are no masters, no servants, no lords, no slaves—all are free, free, as free as their ancestors when they left Egypt. And Itzikl Shostepol sat down to perform the seder ritual with all its splendor and beauty as his father had performed it before him. He chanted the beautiful holiday kiddush as his father had chanted it before him, and he intoned the Haggadah with the same melodies as his father had intoned it before him. When he had finished the service preceding the repast, had washed his hands and made the blessing over the matzo—*Al achilas matzo*—and when they were well into eating the fish—the sugary sweet, peppered and paprika-ed, wonderful-smelling fish, served with broth-softened matzo—Itzikl Shostepol, with an expectant smile, called upon Tamara: "Nu, now you can ask me the Four Questions."

"He's gone out of his mind!" Shivka said to her husband. "The child is still eating and he wants her to ask the Four Questions."

"It's all right, Mama, it doesn't matter. I can eat and ask Papa the Four Questions at the same time," said Tamara to her mother with a smile, and turned to her father, saying, "Father, I want to ask you the Four Questions. Isn't that the way to start the Four Questions?"

"That's the way, that's the way, daughter," her

proud father answered, and her mother's heart swelled with joy.

Tamara went on: "Here we are, celebrating the seder, and as I understand from my Russian Haggadah that you've given me, we are celebrating a holiday of liberation and we hope to be liberated once more from the exile in which we find ourselves now. We hope next year to be free in our own land, in our own Jerusalem. Isn't that so? Let me ask you: First, tell me, what have we been doing to hasten this liberation? I mean, you and I and your parents and our great-grandparents, from their time until this day? Second, I would like to know whether all Jews all over the world desire the Messiah to come to lead us to the Promised Land? Or are there those, and perhaps many, who don't have the least desire to welcome the Messiah, who would remove them from a civilized country and from their fine homes and force them to leave behind the advantages of wealth in order to take them off to a country that is inferior to our own land and suffers under a government even more despotic than our own? Don't interrupt me, Papa—I've only asked you two questions so far, and I have to ask you four. So I have two more to go. Third, I want you to tell me truthfully, isn't the story about Moses and Jerusalem nothing more than an old prayer from an old prayer book that was at one time, years ago, written for the benefit of our great-great-grandparents? And fourth, if that's the way it is, why do we still need this whole comedy nowadays? I hope my foolish questions haven't offended you or spoiled your holiday. I hope you can provide me with an explanation.

To say that the father couldn't answer the daughter's Four Questions would not be altogether correct. Itzikl Shostepol *did* answer them at great length and with

great fervor, gesticulating, as was his manner, and inci-
dentally chiding his daughter for calling the holy seder
of this sacred holiday a "comedy." He flared up, rushing pell-mell over his words, hardly finishing one word
before he was onto the next. In short, Itzikl Shostepol
justified himself as well as he could—unsystematically,
like a person unaccustomed to debate. Such a person
does the best he can—twisting and turning, delivering a
blow from behind, tripping over himself and falling,
springing up and going on. Such a person cannot win
the "battle." Such a man, no matter how hearty and
strong, has to lose.

Tamara allowed her father to rant on, looking at him
with her large lovely intelligent eyes as he became en-
tangled in his own arguments. A faint smile played on
her lovely troubled face, upon which her mother could
not gaze enough. Shivka felt pride and a rare feeling of
triumph. That's the way! Let him know! Let him answer to his own daughter! He thinks she's like me! Ah,
may she just be well, and may she soon be home for
good so she can handle him for me too!

Itzikl glanced at Shivka's face and sensed at once that
she was feeling triumphant over him. He immediately
interrupted himself and exclaimed, "Well! We can sit
here arguing and babbling until morning. We must get
back to the Haggadah and finish the other half of the
seder."

Sasha Safranovitch hated to relax, to sit idle. No
sooner had he stepped down from the carriage than he
let all his friends know he was home. Soon they all
started to come by—old friends and acquaintances,
Zionists, modern enlightened intellectuals, teachers,
and just plain people, most of them poor.

Naturally the pharmacist wasn't too enthusiastic

about these visitors, but he was afraid to protest, as he wished to avoid a conflict with his son. A minor conflict had already occurred between them when Sasha had changed his clothes for yomtov. The father had wanted to show off to his son that he wasn't a provincial, that he read all the Petersburg dailies, and that he participated in the freedom movement. In fact, he himself did nothing—where would he find the time? But he sympathized.

"Do you also sympathize with the liberation of our own people?" Sasha asked him, combing his red hair.

"What people?" his father asked him, and the son answered, "Our own Jewish people."

"Are we also a people?" the father asked naïvely, and the son fixed unbelieving eyes on him.

"What are we, then?"

"How should I know what we are? We're Jews."

And both of them, father and son, burst out laughing.

"I hope you won't be offended, Papa, at what I will tell you," Sasha said to his father.

"Say it, say it, you know me, I'm not one of those who is easily offended. You can say whatever you wish. You'll most likely say that . . . What will you say?"

"I will say to you that you can find no other people in the world that would deny their own existence, that would say of their own people that they are not a people."

"Well, yes!" the pharmacist exclaimed triumphantly in a shrill voice. "Do you know why? Because that's the kind of people we are!"

"Only slaves think that way," Sasha said with disappointment. "Slaves who have altogether lost their identity and their self-esteem under the iron rod of their persecutors."

A debate ensued that lasted a full hour, in which the

father realized how weak he was. He felt the way an adult might feel who is pressed to the earth under the foot of a child.

Pesach evening, just before the first seder, when the pharmacist returned home from the pharmacy, he found visiting his son a scrawny young man whose jacket was out at the elbows. By his curly black hair and stooped shoulders he recognized Sasha's Gymnasium classmate.

"My friend Shimon Kessler." Sasha introduced him to his father, and the pharmacist offered two fingers of his cold pharmacist's hand and said, "My pleasure."

Sasha could tell from his father's sour expression that this Kessler was not a welcome guest, so he hastened to enrich the introduction.

"Kessler, you should know, is an engineer [Kessler moved up at least fifty points in the pharmacist's eyes!] and a noted mathematician [Kessler's stock rose another forty points!] and what's more—a celebrated Zionist! [Here Kessler's stock suddenly plummeted the whole ninety points all at once!] I figured, Papa, you wouldn't mind if my friend Shimon stayed with me over Pesach."

Naturally the pharmacist said he would be happy to have his son's friend stay for Pesach. And so it happened that our new acquaintance, Shimon Kessler, became a resident, a part of the pharmacist's household.

After a lengthy debate through the mail, with letters flying back and forth, Sasha had, as usual, prevailed over his father to make *this* Pesach a real Jewish Pesach, with matzos, kosher dishes, a seder with all its many rituals. In previous years the pharmacist had been content just to buy matzos, solely to please the baker, who was a good customer of his and who kept pestering him to order matzos from him erev Pesach and not from anyone else. For the same reason, on the Greek Orthodox Easter he felt obliged to buy a large, impressive Easter bread for his table to satisfy the German woman who was his housekeeper. There you have a person who didn't want to offend anyone!

The threesome sat down to the first seder—the pharmacist, Sasha, and his friend Shimon Kessler. The father looked out of place in his own house, like a guest. He had put on a black morning coat buttoned to the top, had closed all the shutters so that no passerby could, God forbid, see that Safranovitch the pharmacist was celebrating the seder. He was constantly raising the top hat and mopping the sweat from his brow, complaining that he wasn't used to sitting inside with his head covered. Not until he had sent off his German housekeeper was he able to relax. He simply couldn't abide having his servant see him, the intelligent Safranovitch, taking part in a Jewish seder.

3

The Shoemaker's Pesach Guest

If the beloved Pesach holiday is a delight for the rich, it is Paradise itself for the poor.

An impoverished craftsman, a teacher, a shopkeeper, a tradesman, or a peddler who is bent under the yoke all year round and knows no pleasure except for the one day of Shabbos, when he can allow himself to sleep the day through, hardly knows how to thank God enough when the beloved Pesach arrives and he can rest for eight days in a row, not having to worry himself about how to put food on the table, because matzos have been provided for the entire week. And if God has helped out, and along with the matzos there is a little sack of potatoes and a small crock of Pesach borscht—*then* Rothschild can keep his Paris; no one would change places with him, and certainly not Nehemiah the shoemaker.

The day before erev Pesach, Nehemiah the shoemaker delivered the shoes Shivka Shostepol had ordered, and his two boys delivered their orders to other rich customers. All three bought home pockets full of money. There was more than enough for the four goblets of wine, enough to redeem the holiday clothes from the pawnbroker, and even a few groschen left in the pocket as well. *Now* let Rothschild try to change places with Nehemiah the shoemaker!

Nehemiah's two sons, Chaim and Benny, really worked more for their father—"the old man," as they called him—than they did for themselves. They spent little on themselves. What did such sturdy lads need? Nothing much at all: a suit, a pair of boots, a cheap collar, and a tie, and they were all set, unless there was a meeting, a book to buy, or a friend in need—then a bit more was required. They both enjoyed reading forbidden books. Both were comrades to be counted among the *real* comrades. But the older one was more committed to the Party's philosophy than was the younger. The younger one, Benny, only paid lip service to the philosophy. But the older one, Chaim, was one of their best workers. It would happen on occasion that Chaim would disappear for a day or two; no one knew where he had been or whom he had been with or what he had been doing. The first time this happened his mother nagged his father to do something. "Shlimazel! What kind of a father are you?" The father complained to his good friend Yudel Katanti, "What can I do, my friend?" To this Yudel Katanti replied, "Let him run, Nehemiah, there is nothing you can do about it. Nowadays it's become such a world that the eggs are smarter than the chickens. I have the same problem with my Binyamchik'l. I plead with him as I would with a thief. 'Binyamin,' I say to him, 'it's a pity on you!' He listens to me the way Haman listens to a Purim noise-maker . . ."

And Yudel Katanti put two fingers to his lips signaling for Nehemiah to be silent, and Nehemiah agreed with him and was silent. He asked God for two favors only: that Chaim shouldn't get into trouble and that he shouldn't ruin his younger brother, Benny.

As the younger son, Benny was his father's favorite, while to his mother he was more precious than life itself. He was as pampered as an only child. Although he truly loved Benny, Chaim would tease him, calling him "Buntzi," a girl's name. Of course Benny resented this name and would not tolerate it, but all the same he was prepared to lay down his life for Chaim.

That's the kind of family they were.

"Boys, to work!" announced Nehemiah, which was intended to mean that it was time to prepare for the seder, and Nehemiah put his shoemaker's tools aside. And they all began the seder preparations—Nehemiah, Zissel, Chaim, Benny, and their Pesach Guest, a dark-haired healthy youth, as hairy as a bear, with a basso voice that boomed out like a bell. The Pesach Guest had been brought home by Chaim, as much a stranger as if he had been invited while passing on the street. Actually, a comrade had whispered in Chaim's ear, "He is an escapee. Take him home with you and teach him to be a shoemaker." Chaim looked him over carefully and liked him. He didn't ask his name but just inquired, "What shall we call you?"

"Call me Mischa Neiditch," the escapee boomed out in his basso voice.

Nehemiah the shoemaker couldn't accept this. "What do you mean he wants to be called Mischa Neiditch?" And he started grilling Mischa. "Where do you come from? What do you do for a living? Are you married?" and so on, as one would with a stranger. But his son Chaim interrupted him. "That's no one's business, old man! Better ask him if he wants to eat, or perhaps we should go to the bathhouse first?"

It was decided that they would first go to the bathhouse, and all four—the father, his two sons, and the Pesach Guest—went off to the bathhouse.

Afterward they came back home and sat down to the seder to recite the Haggadah. Only the old man recited, and the others listened, each one following in his own Haggadah.

"Haven't we said enough prayers already?" the shoemaker's older son, Chaim, said, shutting his Haggadah. Following his example, the younger brother, Benny, and the Pesach Guest also shut their Haggadahs, and so did Nehemiah the shoemaker. They all felt starved after the long day of not eating and after the hot baths. Besides, marvelous aromas were wafting from the hearth, teasing their noses—inviting aromas of hot, peppery gefillte fish, of fresh dumplings made with chicken shmaltz, and other such delicacies especially prepared for Pesach and tasting of Paradise itself. Before long the crackle of dry matzo being crunched by strong, healthy teeth was heard, and the first wave of hunger was allayed. After downing two of the four goblets of wine the silent guest spoke up, saying it had been a long time since he had tasted Pesach wine and Pesach fish and Pesach dumplings, because he had spent most of his life in city jails and state prisons.

"How many prisons have you been in?" asked Nehemiah, who was not yet feeling the influence of the wine but was nevertheless feeling mellow.

"I've lost count," answered the Pesach Guest in his deep voice, and Nehemiah added quickly, "Just like Gedalyeh-Leib the thief, blessed be his memory, he's already passed over to the Real World. Gedalyeh-Leib

used to say to himself, 'When they put me in jail, I don't
cry—I know I'll get out. And when they let me out, I
don't dance either—I know they'll put me back in
again!'"

"Shlimazel!" interjected the shoemaker's wife, Zissel,
good-naturedly. "You'd better see to it that our Pesach
Guest should take a little something in his mouth."

But the Pesach Guest had already taken "a little something in his mouth," had already emptied the fifth of the
four goblets of wine too, and was feeling so good and
warm that his tongue loosened and he boomed out in
his basso voice, "If you like, I will tell you the story of
my last escape from prison."

"Are you saying that escaping from prison is no great
event for you? It sounds again like what Gedalyeh-Leib
the thief, may he rest in peace, said," commented
Nehemiah, and his wife, Zissel, cut in, "Shlimazel!
How about keeping quiet for a change?"

"I'm keeping quiet, like a fish!" the shoemaker said to
her.

And they all listened to the story of the Pesach Guest's
last escape from prison.

"For me escaping from prison, my dear friends, is
naplyevat!—I spit on it!" Thus the Pesach Guest, the
hairy Mischa Neiditch, began his tale in his deep bass
voice, which boomed out like a bell.

"I've escaped, my dear friends, not just from prison
but also from Siberia. Not once, but twice. I've hidden
in a butcher's wagon, the meat on top, me underneath.
I've gone on foot with pilgrims a thousand versts, walking for three days straight without food, freezing, without boots—*naplyevat!*—I spit on it! It hasn't harmed me
one bit. Disguised myself if I had to—that I can do too.
My biggest problem is my voice. It's a little too low.

But I'm only talking about provincial prisons. Nothing to it. Not so in the state prison. Once they get you there, they keep you there for good! You might as well say goodbye. When I got into the prison I planned to talk things over with a couple of my comrades—not a chance! They don't allow you to see each other. Talking—impossible, unless you tap on the wall.

"Found out that in the cell next to mine was someone I knew. Her name was Masha—an activist, a leader, and a very, very important person. They wanted to get her out more than life itself, even had a plan for her escape. Communicated with her through the wall. Without warning I was suddenly moved to another section. Bitter! Three days passed. Found out from friends that Masha was also with us. Bravo! Began to worry—a big problem—she was in solitary. Do you know what that means? Four bare walls, not even a place to hang yourself. Cut off from the whole world. Bitter! And I had my own problems. Day after day they dragged me off to be grilled. They wanted to find out who I was. They wanted to know what I'd done. But I don't talk so easy. Beaten like a dog. Did you get a good look at my body in the bathhouse? Do you see this broken finger? Do you see these three knocked-out teeth? *Naplyevat!*—I spit on it!

"Yes, my dear friends! It's a great cause but not an easy one. The thought of escaping was always on my mind. Never mind eating. Who cared about sleeping? I had to escape. And not alone. With her, with Masha! But how? It was driving me crazy. Where had all my comrades gone? Close friends, true comrades, put away in jail, many of them sent off to Siberia. Especially after Bloody Sunday! Every day at dawn they were hanging people—that we knew. Every day we found out that one or two of our comrades had been hanged. No one asked who. Every one of us asked only 'When's my turn?' A knock on the door—a knock in the heart. A rattle of the keys—the blood curdled. Tphoo! May the devil take it!

"I have never been as jumpy as I was then. Nervous! Never knew of nerves. Once—it was in the middle of the night, dark, quiet. Little by little you could begin to hear the tk-tk out in the prison yard. That was the guard pacing up and down over the cobblestones. Suddenly I heard the sound of footsteps. Many footsteps. What could it be? Keys were rattling. Voices could be heard. A lantern light shone into my cell and then vanished. Scrp-scrp! The long iron bar was being unbolted. The door creaked open. On the threshold stood our guard. The lantern light illuminated his frozen face. Behind him the prison patrol and several more guards.

"'Get your things together. Get a move on!'

"Thought to myself, This is a greeting from the Angel of Death. Put my boots on. We went. It was a waste of time even to try to ask them questions—they were mute. A long walk down the corridor. We were in the prison yard. A cold blast of fresh air. Bathed myself in the cool air like in a tub. We crossed the prison yard. The guards paced, staring at us distantly with expressionless eyes. They weren't seeing a human being led to the gallows. They were thinking only of a good night's sleep. We were now in the second prison yard. There was the administrative office and that's where the chief guard lived. He had a wife—I'd seen her. Her face told you she was not really in a prison. The prison was for her a large cage, the prisoners, geese. Every day new geese arrived. You fed the geese and then sent them off to be slaughtered. Who cares about that? Who has pity on a goose? That's why they are geese—so they can be slaughtered. Who can condemn a slaughterer? That's why he is a slaughterer—so he can slaughter. She had a child, a little boy of five, named Vanya, as I heard his nurse calling him. The nurse was likely Polish. I could tell by her hair and by her eyes. Nice hair, blue eyes. She had a voice like a violin. When she said 'Vanya,' she sang it in a somewhat nasal tone. What could Vanya be thinking about those geese-people who were imprisoned there? Did he know that they were *people* locked up there, not geese? What did the governess tell him? She must know. She must have seen tears sometimes. She must have heard screams sometimes. And the clanging of heavy chains—what could this mean to her? Who knows, maybe she herself had a brother who was somewhere in jail, with a gallows waiting for him? Who knows? Now she slept in the house on a soft bed, Vanya next to her in a crib. Someday he will grow up and they will tell him that his father was a hangman. What will Vanya say then? Or perhaps he will also be a hangman like his father.

"I've wandered off. Where was I? At the chief guard's house. Only two windows were lit up. Through the window I could see a tall figure in an officer's uniform—big whiskers, gold-framed spectacles. According to the epaulets, he must have been a captain or a lieutenant. Sat with his legs crossed, smoking a cigarette. Across from him, a clerk bent over a document. On the little porch, five unfamiliar soldiers, all sitting in different postures. One took a cigarette from his sleeve, swallowed the smoke so it couldn't be seen. They talked to each other quietly. A driver gave a signal and soon the clopping of horses was heard. Wheels rolled. The all-too-familiar large prison wagon drove right up to the porch. On the driver's seat I recognized Selivan, the coachman. An ex-convict, a well-known villain. From a distance I saw our chief guard coming with his men.

The keys clinked together. The five soldiers sprang up. Attention!! They brought more prisoners over to the prison wagon. I looked closely at them—two familiar faces. One was Masha, the other a young man of nineteen with soft pink cheeks, hardly out of his baby fat, called Avrutis. Another one—an unfamiliar prisoner. A day or two before, Avrutis had found out that he was being accused of some terrible crime that would probably be the end of him. He's a fine fellow. He behaves as he should. But he had turned a bit pale in the last two days. The color was all gone from his soft cheeks and somehow he seemed to be drawing his coat too tightly around himself. Because it was cold outside? Or maybe because he was saying goodbye in his thoughts to his mother? He has a mother who loves him very much. I once saw her loving letters to him. An ocean of mother love, a world of feeling. A flood of tears. He pretended to make fun of her letters. But when he sat down to write her a letter he couldn't be torn away. He wrote her in verse. He is a poet. Doesn't write badly. At that moment he was so drawn into himself he didn't notice me. But Masha—she saw me right away. She took a step toward me. I looked at Masha, I wanted to see how she was doing. I could barely see her face. She appeared calm—*naplyevat!*

"'*Stroya!* —March!' A voice was heard. The five soldiers marched out single file. They surrounded us. Our chief guard went with the captain out on the porch. The clerk lit the way for them. The captain and the chief guard shook hands, and then the chief guard bowed humbly, very humbly. He begged the captain to forgive him because it had taken so long. The captain was stern. He told him to be more careful next time. 'The General hates delays!' The chief guard was apologetic. He bade the captain goodbye one last time. He told him to be very, very careful with this gang he was delivering and with the "bear." He meant me. The captain told him not to worry, he was not afraid of any bear. No one escaped from him.

"We were soon sitting in the prison wagon. We, together with four of the soldiers with bared swords, sat on the inside front benches. In the second compartment of the wagon was the captain. On the driver's seat Selivan sat with a soldier. The small iron doors slammed shut. I heard one last 'Smirna!' Selivan smacked his lips. I heard the clopping sounds of four pairs of hoofs. The wheels rolled slowly over the cobblestones. Outside the prison walls Selivan gave the horses their heads. The wheels spun faster. The wagon flew noisily over the stones.

"We sat on the two long benches across from one another. Next to each one was a soldier with a bared sword. I looked at Masha. She didn't take her eyes off the young Avrutis. Talking was forbidden. Where we were going none of us knew, but everyone knew it wasn't to a party. This was the way calves were taken to slaughter. Did *they* feel anything? Didn't know how long we were riding. At times it felt like a minute, at times like a whole night. A night—a year.

"Suddenly—stop! The wagon came to a halt. It was quiet. We heard the horses snorting, lashing with their tails. The captain's voice was heard. He had jumped out of the wagon. He was now behind us. He was shouting angrily at the driver. Selivan clambered down from the driver's seat, cursing, and asked what the matter was. 'Don't you see what the matter is? Are you blind? Bend down. Look at this!' ordered the captain. What could it be? A thought occurred to me. Ach, if only an axle would break! Or if some other catastrophe would occur! We would have some confusion, a bit of a riot. Ach, we would jump those soldiers and strangle them one at a time. I myself would undertake to strangle three of them, like kittens. But the soldiers were apparently aware of our thoughts. They sat sternly with their bared swords. Their eyes didn't leave us. Suddenly we heard something fall to the ground. After the fall we heard a hoarse cry. Someone said, 'Tie him up! Like this! The sack over his head . . . That's the way, that's the way . . . Let's grab him . . . Comrades, into the wagon . . . That's the way, that's the way . . .' Before we could look around, the iron doors of the wagon opened. A heavy bundle was tossed into our compartment. In a moment three soldiers were sitting on top of the sack. The captain jumped in with us. He tore off his large mustache and the gold-framed spectacles. He called out to us, 'Comrades! I greet you. You are free!'

" 'Grisha!' I cried out.

" 'Shh!' He signaled to me, pointing to the sack."

Nehemiah the shoemaker turned to look at his children. His nose was red and glistening. He brought his fist down on the table and exclaimed, "I knew it—as I am a Jew, I knew it was a setup!"

"Shlimazel! So why didn't you say anything?" said his wife, Zissel, who was also beside herself with excitement. Chaim and Benny—they, one could say, were transported, carried away by the account. They pictured themselves there together with the Pesach Guest, Mischa Neiditch, in that prison wagon, and they were burning to know the end of the story. Who was this Grisha? And where was Masha? And what finally happened to the young Avrutis and the other prisoners?

The Pesach Guest cleared his throat and went on.

"So where was I? Yes—Grisha. I recognized him. Do you want to know who he is? It isn't important. He's a

143

friend of mine. That's all you need to know. Meanwhile
I have to finish telling you about the prison wagon. The
prison wagon went on farther, driven by the soldier,
also one of ours of course. Selivan lay tied up in the sack
like a ram, with a cloth stuffed in his mouth to shut him
up. Two soldiers (also ours) sat astride him. It was a
problem what to do with him. Kill him? That wouldn't
do. Grisha had said, 'Not a drop of blood!' One soldier
even cracked a joke, 'If we strangle him, no blood
would be spilled.' But Grisha gave him a look and he
shut up. For Grisha you have to have respect.

"But let's get back to our own people. Whoever
hasn't seen the young Avrutis has never seen joy before.
Joy, happiness, heaven, Paradise—all these are weak
words. He sang, wept, kissed everyone—each and
every one. A corner of the sky was already lightening
and day was beginning. We kept on riding. Comrades
were waiting for us at an inn on the outskirts of the city.
They had clothing, food, passports, and money ready
for us. From there we would slip into Finland and from
Finland it was *naplyevat*. Our wagon drove into a large
courtyard. At the far end, hidden by trees, was a white
house. Behind it a garden. In front a stable. There we
stopped. All our comrades came running toward us.

"That's when it really became a kusherei—kissfest.
Grisha didn't allow the celebration to go on too long.
We all changed our clothes. The prison garb and the
soldiers' uniforms were thrown into the wagon. Selivan
was placed on top of the clothes. He was warned not to
dare utter a peep. They needn't have bothered. He was
securely bound hand and foot, his head covered with a
sack and held fast to the wagon. He couldn't have ut-
tered a peep if he'd tried.

"Hunger suddenly grabbed us. How had we worked
up such appetites? Potato dumplings, sardines, sau-

sages. We stuffed ourselves. Grisha didn't let us linger. He rushed the life out of us. He distributed our passports, money, and escape routes—everyone had his own escape route. Masha, Avrutis, and I were to start off together. We took leave of the others, exchanged addresses. One at a time we left the courtyard. Grisha was the last to go.

"The sun rose quickly. The snow sparkled and crunched under our feet. We walked along slowly, the three of us, dressed like laborers. I was a woodchopper, with an axe across my back. Avrutis, a bricklayer, his clothing caked with lime. Masha was dressed like a peasant girl, with beads, brown shoes, a green kerchief, and a rooster under her arm for market. Grisha spent more time on her appearance than on the rest of us. He checked the green kerchief, the brown shoes, the beads, and the rooster, and was satisfied.

"The three of us had to stay together but walk on singly. We had to behave as if we didn't know one another, yet we all had to keep to the same route. We met workers on the way who greeted us. Droshkys and coaches passed by. We didn't dare hire a droshky. Workers don't travel by droshky. We had to go a long stretch on foot, but it was safer. We hadn't as yet seen a streetcar.

"Then a streetcar did come by and stopped. The three of us climbed to the top deck. The proletarians travel upstairs. The streetcar was making its stops, passengers getting off and others getting on. Not far from Ochtinska Street a man got on, a quite ordinary little man. He was wearing gray-tinted eyeglasses. He sat down opposite us, a cigarette between his lips, threw icy glances toward us, and looked away. Suddenly I noticed that the man with the gray-tinted eyeglasses was looking a little too hard at Masha. Masha herself was unaware she was being stared at. For me to tell her this was out of the question. The streetcar stopped. The man with the gray-tinted eyeglasses got off. A heavy weight was lifted from my heart. We rode farther. I told Masha about the person with the gray-tinted eyeglasses. Masha had a good laugh. 'He wasn't looking at me,' she said, 'but at the rooster.' At that moment the tram came to a sudden stop and in a split second the same man with the gray-tinted eyeglasses was standing there. My blood turned cold. Behind him stood police officers and soldiers. They all descended on Masha. Avrutis and I sat frozen in a corner. What could we do? If I jumped up, both of us would be goners!

"We looked on as cold-bloodedly as we could manage. And Masha? She never gave us so much as a single glance. She was afraid her glance might give us away too. Quietly, slowly, meek as a lamb, she got off the streetcar with them. The tram went on its way. The two of us sat there in a state of shock. We didn't even dare turn around to see where the unfortunate Masha had disappeared to. We said not a word. We didn't look at each other. What that young fellow was thinking I can't say. At that moment I felt great hatred toward him. I was disgusted with him! I was sick and disgusted with myself as well. After all, how could I just sit there so calmly while Masha's life was in such danger?"

"Where is she from and who is she, this Masha?" Benny asked him.

"Where she's from I don't know," the Pesach Guest answered. "I only know she is called Masha, and her family name is Bashevitch."

"Bashevitch!" they all cried at once.

"Bashevitch—what of it?" asked the Pesach Guest.

"A fine story but a short one!" said Nehemiah the shoemaker. "Hard to believe, but I know her father.

Lippa Bashevitch is his name, he's called the wood hauler. I saw him just before the holidays right here on these very steps! He was on his way to ask after any news from Petersburg from our wealthy neighbor's daughter, Tamara."

"Tamara?" The Pesach Guest now asked with keen interest. "Who is this Tamara? Not Shostepol?"

"Certainly Shostepol. What of it?"

"Do you know her?"

"Do I know her? How about that! She lives right upstairs!"

"A night of wonders!" said the Pesach Guest, and told how he had met Tamara Shostepol—at Masha Bashevitch's, in fact—and he said he would very much like to see her.

And since everyone at Nehemiah the shoemaker's was feeling tipsy and in high spirits after the ninth of the four goblets of wine, it was agreed not to wait till morning but to go that very moment, right then and there, to inform Tamara that an old friend wished to see her. And Chaim and the Pesach Guest led the way up the stairs.

Itzikl Shostepol had long since finished the *Chad Gadyo* and the Song of Songs but was still presiding regally at the table, smoking, drinking tea, and talking sadly about the Kishinev pogrom, about which the evil-doers were boasting, while the local anti-Semitic sheets were threatening that the same deed would be enacted in every Jewish city as in Kishinev. The anti-Semites were boasting that they would take revenge on the Jews for the revolution that was supposedly being carried on by Jews. Itzikl's daughter couldn't restrain herself and countered that they were wasting their words. They would do nothing, because in order to perpetrate pogroms everywhere, they would need many accomplices.

"Of course they would have to hire mercenaries, hooligans, criminals, and drunks!" said the father.

"With hooligans and criminals you won't get very far. You need to have the people, the workers involved," remarked the daughter, and her father answered her, "The people? The workers? Don't worry, just let there be a pogrom and your workers will also fall to the 'work.'"

Itzikl Shostepol felt his temperature rise. He knew that in this case *he* was in the driver's seat. In these matters he was more experienced and understood more than his daughter. But Tamara didn't allow him to enjoy his triumph for too long and answered cuttingly that one mustn't be shortsighted, and one had to know the difference between the "people" and a few dozen agitators or hired hooligans in Kishinev who had fallen upon a town of helpless people—cowards, women, and children—who had allowed themselves to be massacred and then had gone crying to their relatives and complaining to God, as the great Jewish poet Bialik had described so movingly.

"Have you ever read Bialik?" Tamara asked her father, and received in reply, "Which Bialik? From the mill?"

"The *poet* Bialik," said Tamara. "Don't you know Bialik's poems?"

"What am I, an old woman that I should be reading little ditties by some Bialik, a ditty writer?" said Itzikl Shostepol in all naïveté and seriousness.

Tamara lost all desire to discuss anything further with her father. She pondered the paradoxically unnatural position of the Jews: a people noted for their intellectuals, a literate people, all of whom could read, even women—a people that considered themselves smarter than all other peoples, smarter and better and more pious, and yet when it came to one of their own national poets, that poet was referred to by her knowledgeable father as a "ditty writer." And had it not been for the pharmacist's son, Sasha, she herself would never have known of the existence of a Jewish poet by the name of Bialik. And was she the only one? She knew many like herself who to that very day did not know who Bialik was. It was unimaginable that even an uneducated Russian peasant would not know who Pushkin was. Or that there existed a Pole, for instance, who did not know who Mitzkevitch was. And she came to the conclusion that either Bialik wasn't a poet or we weren't a people, and if we weren't a people, what were we then?

"The shoemaker's son and another person are asking to see you," announced the housemaid, and before they could turn around, Chaim, the shoemaker's son, and the hairy Pesach Guest appeared in the doorway. All three Shostepols reacted with astonishment. What was the neighbor's son doing there right after the seder? Itzikl thought, The nerve of that shoemaker boy! Shivka Shostepol was simply frightened by the hairy being; they had just been talking about hooligans, and—who could say—this might be one of them. Tamara immediately recognized that hairy person to be Berezniak, whom she had gotten to know at Malkin's commune.

She welcomed Mischa Berezniak as cordially as one would an old friend. The apartment was thrown into confusion, in the midst of which something of an incident occurred. Chaim, the shoemaker's son, and the hairy visitor, Berezniak-Neiditch, without asking permission or waiting to be asked, seated themselves, spread themselves out as they would in their own homes, lit up cigarettes, and began conversing with Tamara as an equal!

That brazen shoemaker boy! Barging in with his boots into other people's living rooms! God in heaven, you have to give up your own home! One isn't even master of his own house any more! Itzikl Shostepol was indignant, and Shivka wrung her hands. What was this world coming to! What was happening to the children? Whoever heard that on a holiday, Pesach, right after the seder, some bedraggled paupers should come in and sit down in a room with their daughter and whisper together? It really must be the end of the world!

It was also the "end of the world" for Tamara. From her old acquaintence she found out much, much tragic news—that Masha was in prison, that this one had been exiled, another was going to be exiled, and that Romanenko had that very day been caught and would be hanged.

The first night of Pesach was a quiet spring night, quiet and warm. Still and dreaming, the houses stood deep in sleep. Like sentries on duty the trees were arrayed on either side of the street—barren, leafless trees about to don their green summer garb. From the vast starry sky the moon, wearing a silvery smile, peered down as it moved at a leisurely and majestic pace, every now and then stepping behind a grayish puff of cloud, as if immersing itself in it for a moment, and then emerging into the open expanse of sky, surrounded by small sparkling stars that shimmered and winked, seeming to exchange glances and to whisper among themselves of God and his multitudinous worlds, his billions of planets. All things were asleep on that spring night, on that first night of Pesach.

Only one window in one house on Vasilchikover

Street was open that night and only one person was awake. Tamara stood and gazed out of the open window at the bright silvery moon and the billions of twinkling worlds called stars. Her eyes were dry, her heart turned to stone, her mind confused. She was not stirred by the vast, wondrous universe. And the distant, infinite heavens were alien to her. The earth itself was desolate, and all around her was bleak and empty. A shuddering loneliness, a wild grief, and a cold fury gripped her soul in a tonglike vise, and all she wanted to do was scream, scream, scream.

4

Itzikl Shostepol at His Wits' End

Since Tamara's return from Petersburg, Itzikl Shostepol
had not had a peaceful moment.

The unhappy father found it hard to swallow the
pharmacist's son's habit of visiting his home whenever
he pleased. Always elegantly dressed, he would remove
his gloves, offer his hand to Itzikl Shostepol and to
Shivka, and would dispose himself as if he owned the
place. And to top it all, Shivka herself was beginning to
speak up for her daughter, finding merit in the pharmacist's son, praising him, saying he was a fine young
man. Amazing! Since his daughter had returned from
Petersburg his home had become a different home, his
life a different life, and even his wife a different wife. It
was not the same Shivka as before! She used to have
respect for him, tremble in her shoes, go along with
everything he, Itzikl, said. Now she had become her
own person! She even had her own opinions about people. To her the pharmacist's son was a fine young man!

"I wouldn't be surprised if you'd want me to make a match with that traif'nik the pharmicist!" Itzikl said to his wife jokingly, and was answered by her with a question, as usual.

"Why not?"

"Maybe they've already decided on it?" Itzikl asked further.

"How do I know they haven't?" Shivka answered in the same manner, a question with a question.

"Maybe before long we'll be receiving a mazel tov?"

"Why not?"

"It seems to me I should know that before you, don't you think?"

"Where is it written?"

"Enough of this!"

No father should suffer as much as our unfortunate Shostepol suffered whenever he had to talk to that red-headed young man, the pharmacist's son, about Judaism, Zionism, and other such subjects, which he would never have broached.

But at least Sasha could be tolerated. More intolerable was the fact that every day his daughter would disappear for an hour or two. She would dress and leave without saying where she was going. The father had been aware of this for some time. He wanted to ask her but didn't know how to approach her. He had several times asked her directly, "Where are you going?" but had received the reply, "I'll be right back." He tried to find out through his wife, hoping she would know something, but she knew no more than he.

"How can a mother not know where her daughter goes?" Itzikl asked his wife, and immediately received his own question in return: "How can a father not know where his daughter goes?"

Letting his anger out on his wife was something he no longer could indulge in as before. Since his daughter had been living at home the mother had more pride and self-confidence, and both of them, mother and daughter, seemed to have formed an alliance against him. No sooner would he try to pull his old tricks on his wife, like humiliating her, as he used to, than his daughter would step forward and take on her mother's grievance, and quite effectively too.

But Itzikl Shostepol absolutely *had* to know what was happening with his daughter. Why was she going around the house like a shadow? What kind of nonsense was this, leaving every day for two hours without saying where she was going or whom she was meeting? What was weighing on her mind?

And the father took to spying on her. He began following his daughter wherever she went, and he found out. One day as he followed unnoticed behind her he saw her disappear into the courtyard of the teacher Romanenko.

Itzikl Shostepol almost went out of his mind trying to figure it out. What was his daughter doing at Romanenko's? Ugly thoughts, one uglier than the next, flew through his head. He knew his daughter was well acquainted with the young Romanenko. But he also knew that the young Romanenko was not at home, because he was locked up somewhere in prison, and no word had been received from him.

To whom, then, could she be going? To his parents? He knew, however, that Romanenko's father was an anti-Semite. And now came the ugliest thought of all: his daughter was going there *because* he was an anti-Semite! . . . *Because* he was an anti-Semite, he had an eye on her, Itzikl Shostepol's daughter. . . . And that ugly thought was driving the unfortunate father berserk, and he could find no peace until his daughter returned home. And when she returned home he talked with her about various topics, mostly about Jews, gentiles, our beliefs, their beliefs, all the while searching her eyes to see if he could discover in them some hint. But he was wasting his time! Tamara was the same as always, save, perhaps, that her eyes were more pensive than usual, her face paler, and when she was asked a question she would hesitate before replying. Also, when the pharmacist's son visited, she was no longer irritated with him as before but allowed him to speak. In the meanwhile she went about the house with her hands clasped to her bosom, looking at him with a distracted expression that clearly conveyed her thoughts were far, far from there. . . .

Itzikl Shostepol came home one day distraught and agitated because of his tangled business dealings with all the "takers"—the lawyers who kept him dangling and the bureaucrats who were chipping away at his money.

"Where is the child?" he asked his wife.

"How should I know?" she answered in her usual way.

"What do you mean, how should you know?"

"That's right, how should *I* know?"

"Are you a mother or not?"

"So if I'm a mother, how does it follow that I should know?"

"Where is the 'Barishni'?" Shostepol asked a servant.

"The 'Barishni' is in her room," answered the servant.

"In her room?" And he went to his daughter's room, knocked on the door, and heard a voice, "Who is it?"

"It's me!" The father stepped into the room and saw his daughter lying face up on her bed, her hands clasped under her head. Across her chest lay a page of a newspaper. Her eyes were red as if from crying. He approached her and placed his hand on her head.

"What is it, my child?"

"Nothing."

"Aren't you feeling well?"

"My head hurts a little."

"Do you want to see a doctor?"

"No, no! I don't need a doctor!"

Itzikl Shostepol knew his daughter. If she said no it was no.

That same evening, as the sun was setting, tinting the lower part of the sky red, Itzikl Shostepol rang the pharmacist's doorbell. As long as they had been neighbors this was the first time Shostepol had paid a visit to the pharmacist. Answering the ring was a dark-complexioned young man with curly hair and a bent nose. It was Sasha's friend Shimon Kessler.

"Is the pharmacist's son at home?" Shostepol asked him and immediately regretted having rung the bell.

"Sasha?" Kessler responded. "He's here. He's studying. Come in. Sasha! Come here."

The pharmacist's son came in and, surprised to see Tamara's father in his house, became flustered and turned red as a beet.

"I must—I must ask you something," Shostepol said to him, looking at Sasha's friend Kessler. Sasha surmised his friend Kessler was making Shostepol feel uncomfortable.

"Shimon, go out for a while," said Sasha to his friend, and asked Itzikl Shostepol to sit down.

Itzikl Shostepol looked around the room. "Don't you have a separate room?" he asked Sasha.

"Let's go into my study," Sasha said cordially, and led him into his small, neat, bright study. Itzikl looked around the study, which was crammed with books, newspapers, and journals.

Itzikl took a deep breath and said to Sasha, "It's to your credit that you aren't sitting idle. You young people are doing something, are concerned for the Jewish people. We can't, we don't have any time, we're involved, busy night and day, as you can see, with business affairs, making a living, commerce . . ."

"That's exactly the trouble," Sasha said to him. "While you are preoccupied with business affairs, your subcontracting and commissions, the Jewish people are going under."

"Exactly right!" the visitor said, jabbing his finger to indicate he had hit the nail on the head. "Exactly right! May I have such a good year as you are right! I made the same point to my daughter. What good does it do us, I say, to get involved in politics, revolutions, shmevolutions? I hope I'm wrong, I say, but it will surely end up being like Kishinev, with a pogrom and with being driven from the towns and cities, I say. I do business with gentiles and rich people, and they point their fingers at us, saying we are guilty for everything! I say that a Jew shouldn't get involved, a Jew should know that he is a Jew."

"And kiss the rich gentile's hand and grovel before him? Or sit and wait until they come and rip up your pillows, break your chairs, rob you of your savings, torture your wife, rape you daughter?" said Sasha to his guest, and the guest answered him, "Well, well, well! You're the same as all the rest of them! What words you all throw around! Crusade? Struggle? Fighting? I thought you were a quiet type, and look at you. . . . My daughter is also like that."

"The difference between us is that I say we should

crusade for our *own* people, which for me is closer to home, and your daughter has gone far off."

"Yes, my daughter has gone far off, too far!" Itzikl Shostepol said, sighing and smiling bitterly. His large dark eyes expressed his anguish and his voice dropped. "That is the reason I came to see you. First of all, to lighten my heart a little. I recognized you to be a sympathetic person. Please believe me, I like you—that is, I've grown to like you. At least you've retained a bit of Jewishness."

"Thanks," Sasha responded with a curt smile.

"Not at all," Shostepol said seriously. "And second of all, I wanted to show you something. I'll soon show it to you. But first you mustn't think, God forbid, that I'm worried about my daughter. I know my daughter very well, you can take my word for it."

"I believe you."

"So I've made myself clear," said Shostepol and stole a look at Sasha. "What's the problem, you say? It's just that I don't understand her! I don't begin to understand her! You certainly must know my daughter's tutor, the Gymnasium teacher Romanenko's son—a fine gentile, an honest man, but a zealous Party man! One of *those* . . . . My daughter thinks very highly of him. I think highly of him myself, but she—more than anyone! He's a god in her eyes! But I tell you a person is not a god. She says I don't know Romanenko. I say I know greater people than he. I know the state prosecutor, I know the lieutenant governor, I know the governor himself. . . . And she laughs at me. You know, to *them* the governor is traif. But that's not my point. A god is a god. . . . But he isn't here, that god—I mean the young Romanenko—so why on earth is she going there?"

"Where?"

"Do I know where? To his parents, I suppose. You

know his father and what an anti-Semite he is. What can she be doing there every day?"

"Who?"

"My daughter, Tema—I mean Tamara! Till I found out where she was going! Every day, every single day she would vanish for two or three hours, and I didn't know where she was going. I didn't have the faintest idea where she was going, and that's that! Well, to make a long story short, I did find out where she was going. How did I find out? Never mind, as long as I found out. What is she doing there? How should I know what she's doing there? What should I think? How can I explain it? She's a Jewish daughter, they are gentiles, and the father is a dyed-in-the-wool anti-Semite. I know my daughter and I know she hates that old Romanenko the same as I do. How can I say 'hate'? After all, we live in the same neighborhood. So what does he have to do with us? I know he's as traif to her as he is to me. Do you need proof? She herself once told me a story, which I'll tell you in secret, so be sure you don't tell my daughter."

"You shouldn't tell me secrets to keep from your daughter," Sasha said, looking ill at ease.

"Mentsh! It's not a secret! Everyone in Petersburg knows it, all of Petersburg knows! But that's not my point. Ask yourself this question: What business can she have with them?"

"With whom?"

"How do I know with whom? With his parents, I suppose. Picture it. I didn't take my rest, I followed after her, I trailed her, and—I don't know, I don't know anything. I see the child going downhill every day, I can see her anguish. But about what? I don't know and I cannot find out. Today, for example, I came in and found her teary-eyed with a page of a newspaper in her hand. 'What's the matter, child?' 'Nothing.' Now she's gone off there and left behind the newspaper with some lines marked in red. It's a foreign newspaper and I can't read it. I would love to know what it says. I wouldn't trust anyone else, but I do trust you."

"I thank you very much," said Sasha, rattled by this entire conversation, "but I don't feel comfortable becoming involved in your daughter's personal matters."

"What kind of a person are you?" Itzikl Shostepol exclaimed. "Whom else could I tell? Who else can read it for me? Don't forget, it's my one and only child! She's my precious daughter and I love her!"

These last words were spoken with such passion that Sasha Safranovitch took pity on Tamara's father, and perhaps he himself also wanted to know what was written in the newspaper. What person can go past a place where he knows there is a secret and not peek behind the drawn curtain? One also mustn't forget that Sasha Safranovitch had more than a little interest in Tamara Shostepol. If someone else was in love with Tamara, he certainly wasn't more in love with her than Sasha, and certainly not *before* Sasha. And he took the newspaper from the father and read:

> On the tenth, at twelve noon, in the fortress chamber where a certain Romanenko was being held, the State Prosecutor arrived and informed the prisoner that at two o'clock he would be executed by hanging. Not a muscle moved on the doomed man's face. The State Prosecutor handed him a prepared plea for clemency. but the sentenced man categorically refused to sign it and asked for a cup of tea. The State Prosecutor left and then returned, offering him his life if he would sign the document. The sentenced man again told him he would never sign such a plea. When he was asked whether he wished to see a member of the

clergy before his death, he replied that he needed no clergyman or any official representative of a religion. His religion, his credo, was a personal one. His conscience was clear, he knew he had done no wrong. The doomed man emerged from the chamber proudly and calmly, as if he were going for a stroll. When he was led to the scaffold, he turned to an officer, saying gently the following: "Tell my comrades that I die calmly and I will be with them forever." His last words were, "Send my love to my mother!" Such a superhuman calm had never been witnessed within the walls of the fortress. So died a Russian hero.

5

A Quiet Tragedy with a Turbulent Sequel (Taken from the newspapers)

ITEM NO. 1: Prison inmates declared a hunger strike for three days and created a big disturbance following the discovery of a girl who had hanged herself in one of the prisons. The military had to be called in to restore order. Three Bundists were slain, eleven wounded, eight of them seriously.

ITEM NO. 2: The girl who was the cause of the prison uprising was found hanging from the iron bars of her cell window. She had torn strips from a shirt and knotted them together. The reason compelling the girl to commit suicide in prison is even more gruesome than her death.

ITEM NO. 3: We have succeeded in obtaining some

particulars about the hanged girl who was recently found in one of the prisons. This is the account, as told to us by a reliable source: A short time ago several inmates escaped from prison under most unusual circumstances. In the middle of the night the Chief Guard received a phone call in which a certain password was used informing him that an officer with several soldiers would soon be arriving at the prison in a special wagon to remove and transport to the state prison several political prisoners, among them a certain girl, a confessed subversive who had been accused of many crimes. And indeed, in a few minutes the soldiers arrived with the officer, who presented a signed document from the State Prosecutor. In it were listed the same names of the political criminals who had been requested by phone.

In the course of half an hour all the formalities were completed, and the officer together with the prisoners drove off. It was not until the following morning, after the prison wagon had failed to return, that the State Prosecutor was notified by telephone and it was discovered that it had been a trick, a clever hoax perpetrated by revolutionaries.

But that same morning it was the good fortune of an expert police spy to recognize one of the escapees. He arrested her and brought her to the precinct office. From there she was taken to another precinct office, and from there to a third. The following evening they discovered the unfortunate girl hanged. The name of the girl, as we have learned, was Manya, or Masha Bashevitch.

ITEM NO. 4: Today at ten o'clock in the morning several hundred students and ten thousand workers gathered and attempted to hold a memorial service for the hanged Bashevitch. The police quickly appeared and dispersed the crowd. No serious clash occurred. Thirty people were taken to the hospital.

ITEM NO. 5: Two hours later that same day a memorial service was in progress for Masha Bashevitch, at which inflammatory speeches were made and a red flag hoisted. As a result of these provocations the clash with the police was much more serious. Twenty-two were counted dead and more than a hundred severely wounded, among them many women and children. Calm now prevails.

ITEM NO. 6: In the aftermath of the clash at the memorial service for the hanged Basehvitch strikes broke out in several factories, which spread to other cities. A general railroad strike is being planned.

Soldiers have been stationed in all the courtyards and the streets are calm.

Day by day the air became thicker and more suffocating. Heavy clouds covered the sky. The air smelled of sulfur. The storm was drawing ever closer. At any moment one could expect a cloudburst, a downpour, a flood.

If Masha Bashevitch's death provoked such storms elsewhere, one can only imagine what an uproar it provoked in the city where she was born, where almost everyone knew her, where the smallest child could point to her and say "There goes Masha." Lippa Bashevitch's neighbors, who once used to avoid the wood hauler with his wondrous tales about his daughter

Masha, those same good-hearted people suddenly began to take pity on the poor father in his profound, indescribable bereavement, and were eager to console with words what is inconsolable, to heal with a sigh the deep pain that can never be healed. Those good-hearted people, who had never taken an interest in Lippa's daughter, suddenly began to remember the girl with the bobbed hair and her many virtues. Everyone was eager to say at least a comforting word to the bereaved father and at the same time plague him with all kinds of questions. Had he received any letters from her in her last days? What had she written? Was it true, as the papers said, about her escaping from prison, and how had this all come about?

"It seems to me she was just an ordinary girl, a nothing, the same as all the rest," people said. "Who could be a prophet and know that this girl would some day grow up and be such . . . such a . . . so that the whole world would be talking about her!"

When Lippa Bashevitch first learned about the great tragedy he tore out clumps of beard and went berserk, running wildly from the house, his arms outstretched, heedless of where he was running. When he finally returned he flung his boots off, ripped the lapel of his already torn kaftan, as well as tearing his wife's clothing and his children's, as a sign of mourning. They all seated themselves on the ground to sit shivah. Only Alek, a boy of eighteen, refused to sit on the ground. He didn't so much as shed a tear. But his face was ablaze and his eyes were glassy. He checked his trouser pockets for money and said, "Father! I'm going straight there. Please don't try to stop me!"

Neither the father's anger nor the mother's tears nor the younger children's entreaties prevailed. Alek disappeared without a trace. Lippa Bashevitch did not know where Alek had gone. Let him go, he thought. He knew only one thing: he knew he once had had a Masha and now she was no more! Lippa knew that the whole town, the whole world was engrossed with his Masha. Even Itzikl Shostepol, who used to go the other way when he saw him coming, now would stop him whenever he saw him and question him closely about Masha. And that's not to mention Itzikl's daughter! If not for her, he and his wife and his children would have died of hunger.

Even gentiles, pious Christians and students, were holding memorial services throughout the country and locally too. That very day there would be, it was said, a meeting in the Great Shul, a kind of assembly to pray for the souls of deceased relatives. He felt he had to be there even though his wife tried to talk him out of it. She said, "You don't have to go." But what does a woman know? Why should he be deprived of this bit of satisfaction, of hearing what people had to say about his Masha? And Lippa went to the Great Shul, where he saw a huge crowd gathered in the street, the likes of which he had not seen in a long time. Had the biggest millionaire died, so large a crowd would not have assembled! And inside the shul what goings-on! Was it even possible to get in? Would they allow anyone in? It was lucky he was recognized.

"It's the father! . . . Let the father in! . . ."

And Lippa Bashevitch entered proudly, barely pushing himself through to the front of the shul, where Itzikl Shostepol, the Bernsteins, the Halperns, and other important people were seated. He saw before him many familiar faces—Safranovitch the pharmacist, Nehemiah the shoemaker with his boys, Yudel Katanti, and more and more. . . . The synagogue was draped in black, suitable for mourning. Gloom was written on every face, on men's and women's alike. On the dais stood an unfamiliar young man with red hair, most likely a student, if not perhaps the pharmacist's son, making an eloquent speech. Lippa didn't understand him. He spoke well and to the point, but he didn't understand him. He was quoting entire verses from the Biblical "Concubine of Givah," "Sodom and Gomorrah," and the "Generation of the Deluge."

People were wiping their eyes, but he, the father, felt nothing. And even afterward, when the choir began to sing and the chazzan, pursing his lips, chanted his sorrowful, plaintive rendition of *"El m'lo rachamin"*—the Kaddish, the prayer for the dead—and the shul was filled with weeping—young children wept, old men wept, women fainted—he himself did not understand why he felt nothing. But when it came to the words *es n'shamas habasulah Miriam Gilt, bas Reb Lippa halchah l'olamah*—the soul of Miriam Gilt, daughter to Reb Lippa, which enters eternity—the stricken father experienced a tearing away of something in his heart, a suffocating constriction in his throat, a hammer blow directly to his brain, and suddenly ripping from his throat came an inhuman sound as from an ox being slaughtered, an agonized bellow, rising and falling. He himself took fright at this wild sound and chuckled quietly in his beard at his ox voice. And the choir kept on singing and the chazzan kept on pouting and showing off, and poor Lippa felt as if at that moment he had forgotten why he had come there and what the whole crowd was doing there.

And then another person mounted the dais, some unfamiliar hairy, husky man like a bear, with a bearlike voice, and he thundered, "Do you know who Masha Bashevitch was?" At that point Lippa Bashevitch remembered why he had come there and what the crowd was doing there. But he couldn't understand one detail: what was this hairy being saying about his Masha, that she *was*?! What did that mean, she *was*? Nu, where was she *now*? And it was impossible for Lippa Bashevitch to remember where his daughter was. And Lippa Bashevitch couldn't understand what the soldiers were doing in shul. Soldiers riding on horses? Why was everybody running every which way so frantically? Why were people jumping out the windows? Why the stampede? Why the confusion? A blow from a police club stunned him, and he was taken with all the others down to the police station. In the police courtyard their names were taken down. And when his turn came they took him by the scruff of the neck and threw him out.

"Can't you see, the old man's cuckoo?"

"What evil demon drove me to go to shul?" said Itzikl Shostepol after he emerged from the synagogue unharmed, having suffered no more than a glancing blow on the back from a police club. "Luckily I'm the kind of person who doesn't get mixed up in things like that. . . ."

"That you aren't mixed up in things like that is nothing. That our Tema didn't fall into their clutches—*that's* something to be grateful for!" said his wife, Shivka, and thanked God each day, every hour, every minute that her daughter was with her. Her heart told her—a mother's heart knows—that God would not allow her to keep this precious gift for too long. If not today, then tomorrow, God forbid, her child would be snatched from her.

Shivka Shostepol confided these fears to her cook, Chava, the old woman, and no one could understand and sympathize better than Chava, who herself had suffered a disaster, an umglik.

Chava's umglik consisted in her having a son who, all by himself, was an umglik. His name was Shmulik, but she called him "Umglik"—Disaster.

"I know I shouldn't blaspheme, but to deny the truth is also forbidden. To look at him, he's a fine young man—tall, smooth-skinned, lively. And to talk to him, it seems he's no fool either—a quiet, dignified young man and a good worker. Golden hands! He's a clockmaker. His boss, Yossi the clockmaker, can't praise him enough. Really talented! But the devil only knows what's gotten into him. Since he got mixed up with those shoemaker's boys, may they be carried off somewhere, the child has changed completely! In the first place, what business does he have with shoemaker's boys? His father wasn't a shoemaker and his grandfather neither. That wouldn't be so bad if he wouldn't also be reading pamphlets about expro—Tphoo! I've forgotten what it's called! Or if he didn't get mixed up with other people's business, racking his brain over what's happening to other people's workers. What do you care, I say, if someone's workers want to work twelve or fourteen or eighteen hours a day? As far as I'm concerned, they can knock their heads against a wall, together with their bosses, even twenty-six hours a day. What, isn't it so?"

"Definitely so!" said Shivka, looking around to see if Tamara had overheard the conversation. Nowadays everyone had nothing but troubles, troubles, troubles with children.

Earlier, before her daughter had come from Petersburg, she had counted the minutes till she would arrive safely. And when she heard that all the Gymnasia and universities had been shut, Shivka was overjoyed.

"An end to it. She'll stop this studying and maybe we can begin to think of proposing a match for the child. It's high time!

"So it turns out—be a prophet and know—that if she isn't studying, it would be even worse! What can be worse than seeing a child walking around like a shadow, bored, disappearing for two or three hours at a time, who knows where, spending time on idle affairs, carrying on friendships with nobodies like the shoemaker's children? Who knows what's going on with her! The frightful things one hears about these days—killing, shooting, explosions—have become commonplace, and now they're talking of pogroms, of bloodshed! God in heaven, how does one live through such dreadful times?!"

That same night there was a small gathering at Tamara Shostepol's. As soon as evening came she ordered the shutters to be closed and tea to be prepared. At eleven o'clock young people began arriving singly, among them the shoemaker's boys, Yudel Katanti's son, and even that large hairy being, Neiditch. Last but not least, Chava's son, Shmulik, stopped by. During the entire time that the young group was gathering, Itzikl Shostepol could not rest easy but kept shrugging his shoulders, jumping up from his chair, and pacing about the house with his hands clasped behind him, glaring daggers—enraged! But when he spotted the cook's boy coming in he was completely undone and, collapsing on the sofa, grabbed his head and started to rock back and forth, wailing, "My God! My God! My God!"

"Itzi! God in heaven! What's wrong?" Shivka exclaimed, and Itzikl signaled with his finger to his lips.

"Sha! Quiet! Don't yell! You'll *really* get us in trouble! We don't hear anything! We don't see anything! We don't know anything! We aren't even at home— Sh-sha!"

6

A Bitter Time

Nevertheless Itzikl Shostepol had not remained passive. He had taken matters into his own hands. If you have a daughter, a gifted daughter at that, you have to see to it that she is married off, and so a match has to be arranged. But how? Naturally, in the new style, in a modern way, according to the times. The right hand mustn't know what the left is doing. The future couple mustn't know that one day they would be a married pair. The matchmaker must stand on the sidelines, and the young man must get acquainted with the young girl and dance attention upon her until the time is ripe, until the right hour strikes. There is no more charming sight in the world than to see a young man or a few young men dancing attention on a young girl, trying to impress her and outshine the others for her favors.

And dancing their attention on Tamara were some of the finest young men of the city. And while they were dancing attention on such a revolutionary as Shostepol's daughter, they became, as one would expect, passionate advocates of the revolution, tossing about high-flown words and nicely turned phrases. But Tamara Shostepol demanded of these young bourgeois revolutionaries that they demonstrate their sympathy for the cause not merely with finely turned phrases, not merely with high-flown words but with their fortunes. And what did these bourgeois "princes" possess if not money? And what else could one demand from such bourgeois revolutionaries but money? And the bourgeois revolutionaries opened their purses wide and gave money for the revolutionary movement, one more than the next. Tamara demanded no less of them and was satisfied with their friendship, and certainly *they* were satisfied with hers—everyone was happy, and happiest of all was the matchmaker, who was operating behind the scenes. All of his work took place behind the scenes. He would show up once a week in the evening at the Shostepols', exchange a few words with Itzikl Shostepol or with Shivka, inquiring, "Nu? How is it going?"

"Thank the Blessed One, it seems to be coming along," Itzikl would say, and Shivka would add, "If only the Eternal One would wish it, He could make it happen a little faster. . . ."

But the Eternal One was in no rush to make it happen a little faster. The Eternal One has time. And the summer passed, with its long, hot days, and there came a night, a warm, starry summer night with a deep-blue sky and with a singing of birds from a nearby garden. It was a night for lying awake next to an open window, dreaming and weaving golden fantasies. In our Itzikl's head one could discover a weave of wonderful, lofty, precious dreams: a betrothal party . . . a bridal canopy . . . For the Jews a wedding supper . . . For the gentiles a ball . . . And at the ball, many of the gentry, the head of the provisions department, the warden of the prison, two generals, and more of the elite. They are drinking heartily from large tumblers, asking to be introduced to the bride. They praise her to the skies, praise all Jewish girls. All Jewish girls, they say, are pretty, are full of charm—enchanting, enchanting!

Suddenly Itzikl Shostepol heard the doorbell ring. Who could that be, ringing so late? The servants were already asleep. The doorbell rang again and again. He would have to open the door himself. And Itzikl Shostepol took it upon himself to open the door, and there stood Anton Ivanovitch!

Anton Ivanovitch Kholodkov was an old friend of Shostepol's. He had been the local police chief for a great many years and was a good gentile—he always accepted a little something on the side. . . . He and Itzikl Shostepol were quite cozy—he spoke familiarly to Itzikl and slapped him on the back. Every holiday he would stop by the Shostepols' for a glass of wine, praise the fish, and rebuke Shostepol for tolerating such a proud daughter. Whenever Tamara saw him she would hide and refuse to visit with Anton Ivanovitch. Anton Ivanovitch understood the meaning of this and, winking at the father, would say, "You pamper her too much! She is too spoiled! You shouldn't give in to a daughter so much!" While Anton Ivanovitch reproved him for his daughter, Itzikl would swell with pride.

When he saw Kholodkov, Itzikl Shostepol immediately stepped forward to greet him. "Anton Ivanovitch!" And he quickly sprang back, because he saw behind Kholodkov an unknown sergeant and a security officer and several soldiers in addition.

Luckily Itzikl Shostepol wasn't an old woman who fainted easily. He let the police in, bowing and scraping as he invited them to enter. He could have spared himself the effort—they were already inside.

"Where's your daughter?"

Itzikl knew they would be asking for his daughter. For what other reason would such important guests come? He bade them wait till he would awaken his daughter and call her in. They thanked him—it wasn't necessary. They would do it themselves. They started toward the daughter's room. The father gestured helplessly with his hands and trembled.

Shivka had heard unfamiliar voices and had sprung frightened out of bed. "Itzi, what is it?" she cried with alarm.

"Nothing, nothing at all, go back to sleep!" her husband said to her, motioning her back with his hands. But how could she go back, God pity her, when she saw soldiers in her home and her heart told her it was on account of her daughter?

"Itzi! Tell me, what's going on?" the poor woman pleaded with her husband, but her husband kept on waving her away.

Lovely and calm as always, magnanimous as a princess, Tamara emerged from her room. The white kerchief on her just combed hair added even greater charm to her beautiful bright face. With one glance of her large lovely dark eyes she took in the whole scene. Calmly she went over to her parents, who stood frozen with fear and consoled them. "It's nothing, don't get upset. Nothing will happen to me. They won't kill me."

And Tamara embraced her mother, then her father, and kissed them (for the first time that summer). The police officer broke in, saying this was not the time for kissing.

The hand cannot write down in a day what a disturbed, terrified imagination can conjure up in a minute.

There was not a fear or worry in the world that did not occur to the wretched father in those moments when the police and the security officers "did their job," and the thought that was the most frightening of all was that all this had something to do with Romanenko. That single thought alone was enough to turn him cold and hot and cold again.

And when Tamara had left and the receding sound of the coach wheels told Itzikl that his daughter had been taken away—his only child, his one beloved, precious, dear, kind Tamara—then the miserable father began running frantically from room to room, moaning and groaning, wringing his hands, tearing at his hair, banging his forehead against the wall, until at last he collapsed into Shivka's arms and burst into tears. "Doomed! It's all over with our child!"

The first person to whom the miserable father turned was, understandably, Anton Ivanovitch. The police chief, Anton Ivanovitch, was still asleep when Itzikl Shostepol timidly rang his doorbell. He was greeted by a clerk named Netchiporenko and a dog, Sirko. Affecting a servile little smile, he inquired after Anton Ivanovitch and was informed that Anton Ivanovitch was still asleep. He tiptoed after the clerk Netchiporenko into his office, where he slipped him a silver coin. Netchiporenko, a swarthy young man with a flat forehead and heavily pomaded hair, pocketed the coin discreetly, coughed into his hand, and bade Shostepol sit closer to the open window—it was better at the window.

Netchiporenko was right—it *was* better at the window. The summer morning was hot. Outside Kholodkov's window it was verdant and fresh. One could see a small garden with two or three young trees. Onions, salad greens, and bitter herbs were sprouting in the garden. A plump, fluffed-out hen was parading about with her brood of chicks, and the air was filled with her clucking and their peeping. Netchiporenko was writing with a scratchy pen.

Itzikl Shostepol gazed out into the garden and pondered on *olem hazeh*—the ways of this world—which had entirely become the province of Esau. Jacob, who had cheated Esau out of his birthright and of Isaac's blessing, was left with plagues, woes, and pestilence, with pain and searing agony. Here he was, Itzikl Shostepol, a well-to-do Jew, one could even say wealthy, who had but one child. And what pleasure did he have in his life? Had he ever allowed himself to enjoy having such a little garden? Such fresh, green young trees? Hens with little chicks? What did he know about living except for business and business and again business? Except for landowners and landowners and again landowners? How well had this clever Jacob fared in comparison to his simple brother, Esau?

From the other room a familiar voice was heard. "Ne-tchi-po-ren-ko!" It was Anton Ivanovitch waking up, calling for his clerk. Several minutes later Shostepol was called in. Itzikl Shostepol placed a sealed packet on Anton Ivanovitch's table. Anton Ivanovitch glanced quickly at the packet and asked Shostepol, "What's that for?" Itzikl Shostepol did not answer his question but asked him if he had slept well.

For a while the two sat silently. Then the Jew addressed the police chief with a servile half smile: "Anton Ivanovitch must have guessed why I've come. . . . Anton Ivanovitch must know what's going on. . . . I ask nothing from Anton Ivanovitch except one thing—to tell me what's going on. . . ."

"You're a great fool, Shostepolietz! [That's the derogatory manner in which the police chief addressed

176

him.] I'm surprised at you. You're a Jew, aren't you, and the Jews are supposed to be smart. So how come you're asking me about it? Don't you understand that I know as little as you? What do the local police know? A policeman is a broom, a stick in the hands of a higher authority. They tell us to go—we go. They tell us to arrest—we arrest."

"Anton Ivanovitch will at least tell me where she is? Where is my daughter?"

"Your daughter, Shostepolietz, is in prison."

"In prison!"

Itzikl Shostepol felt as if he had been shot in the heart. He broke into a sweat and seemed to shrink by a head.

"If Anton Ivanovitch would be so kind as to tell me, to whom can I go, to whom can I turn?"

"Why don't you go to the warden of the prison?" the police chief responded. "You and he are old friends. You both make it by the fistfuls. [Anton Ivanovitch demonstrated with his hands how they both made fistfuls.] Why don't you go to him? Maybe he can tell you why she's been arrested, though I don't believe anything will come of it. First of all, he knows as much as we do. Only the security police know, and no one else. And second of all, he's a son of a bitch, your warden. Yes, a real son of a bitch!"

"You're absolutely right, he's a son of a bitch!" said Itzikl, standing, straightening up, and letting out a deep sigh. And when he was already standing at the door he received from Anton Ivanovitch yet another scolding for having given in so much to his daughter. Anton Ivanovitch had told him time and time again that one must not indulge a child so much, must not spoil her so.

"Now do you see, Shostepolietz, that I'm a good friend?"

With a feverish head and a chilled heart Itzikl Shostepol ran out and made his way to the warden at the prison.

The prison was like all prisons—depressing, huge, standing mute, many-chimneyed, its walls perforated by many small windows from the roof to the ground floor. It was a monstrous Angel of Death with many eyes. However many times Itzikl Shostepol had been there, he had never given so much as a thought to the souls who were being purified in that purgatory. And even if he did give it a thought, it was but for a fleeting moment. When did he have the time for it? He could never have imagined that those small windows would someday have special meaning for him, that those iron bars, those mute walls would withhold from him what he so much wanted to know. Was it really possible that his daughter was now inside with those for whom he supplied provisions? It couldn't be! It was a dream! A bad dream!

He rode up to the prison, jumped out of the droshky, and rang the bell of the warden's door, which was to the right side of a fence. It was a small white cottage with large flower-filled window boxes. In the window was a green parrot in a gilded cage.

The sentry at the door knew the contractor Shostepol and knew too that a glass of whisky was in store for him. Whenever the Jew came he would slip a silver coin into his hand. For what favors he himself did not know.

"You want to see the warden? Please go into his office. They're inside," said the sentry to him, already holding out his hand to receive the coin, and showed the dealer Shostepol into the warden's office.

The prison warden, Miron Fedeyevitch Kabalkin, was a gentile who had a head for business. No Jew had ever cheated him; and any Jew who thought he *had* cheated Kabalkin realized afterward that *he* was the one who had been cheated. One eye looked upward, while the other eye looked directly into your soul. He had the habit of fiddling with his uniform buttons as he spoke to you, buttoning and unbuttoning them. He spoke rapidly and to the point, hating to waste words. When he saw Itzikl Shostepol in his office he shrugged his shoulders, looked at him with his one direct eye and said, "No, my friend, don't ask me, I don't know anything! I'm busy today and I don't have any time. Please don't be offended."

And poor Itzikl Shostepol had to leave, his heart desolate, once again having to catch sight of the mute walls of that deathlike prison.

Where next? Itzikl wondered, and asked to be taken to the wealthiest part of the city. He got out and rang first the doorbells of those parents whose sons were courting his daughter. They lived like nobility in the finest mansions, naturally directly opposite the governor. Jews looked on them as troublemakers because they aroused envy in the gentiles—and you know gentiles! The gentiles would ask, "Who is in exile, the Jews in our land or we in theirs?"

At the first door he encountered a butler wearing a black frock coat and white tie. Of course he was a gentile and of course a mean one at that, who would allow no Jew across the threshold.

"Wait here!" was his answer to everyone. Itzikl had an idea: he slipped the gentile "squire" at the door half an eagle and told him to tell the Jewish "squire" that *Isak* Shostepol wished to see him urgently. He used those very words—*Isak* Shostepol, pronounced in the Russian way—and it worked! The doors were opened wide for him. He was led into a fine salon, seated on a soft chair, received with very friendly smiles, and was offered tea, which he politely refused. But when the time came to bring up the matter for which he had come, the friendly little smiles vanished.

"What? Your daughter is in prison? What can that mean? Terrible! Terrible! What a blow, like a bullet to the heart! What advice can one give you? Alas, there's nothing we can do. We don't know *that* kind of people."

That was the warm "welcome" Itzikl Shostepol received at the hands of his upper-crust prospective in-laws whose sons were courting his daughter.

The only one who truly commiserated with the disconsolate father in his great anguish and in whom Itzikl Shostepol found a true, devoted friend was, as the reader might have guessed, Sasha Safranovitch.

The pharmacist's son didn't wait until Shostepol came to ask *him* for help. As soon as Sasha heard that Tamara had been taken away in the middle of the night he immediately ran upstairs to Shostepol and found the inconsolable mother, Shivka Shostepol, in such a state that a doctor had to be called to revive her and medicines had to be obtained from the pharmacy. Later, when the father returned from his great success of a trip to his gentile and Jewish good friends and stumbled into the house with an expression on his face that needed no explaining, Sasha responded by volunteering to go wherever it might be necessary. If special influence were needed or family connections, there was a way through his father. The pharmacist knew many Christian officers with whom he played cards.

"Wait!" Sasha cried, slapping his forehead, "I have it! I have it! My father has an acquaintance, an old spinster friend, Nadezhda Alexandrovna is her name. She comes into the pharmacy every day. This Nadezhda Alexandrovna has a brother who is a security sergeant who must know a lot. If you'll give me permission, I'll go right over to Nadezhda Alexandrovna. She thinks highly of me."

"If *I'll* give you permission?" said Itzikl and couldn't go on. If he weren't too embarrassed to do so, he would have thrown his arms around Sasha's neck and kissed him, because he felt he was his friend, a true, devoted friend, the only one among all his good friends.

Sasha left immediately for the old lady's house, and found her in her garden transplanting seedlings. When she saw the young Sasha she rose from her work and greeted him with a fine "Good morning," and chided him for not visiting her more often in her small Garden of Eden with its variety of scented flowers, blossoming young trees, and velvet grass that begged to be stroked. Narrow golden footpaths spread with sand stretched like yellow ribbons over green silk, adorned with flowers by the gentle hand of that fairy princess of this Garden of Eden, Nadezhda Alexandrovna. Unfortunately this fairy princess, her spectacles sliding down her nose, began enumerating in her harsh, mannish voice how much the house had cost and how much the garden brought in. "It isn't profitable, it doesn't even bring in five percent profit." A fairy princess wearing spectacles, talking percent and profit! Ach! What a contrast with the miniature Garden of Eden! Sasha brought up the subject that he had come to discuss.

All the while the young Safranovitch spoke, the old lady stood with her hands clasped behind her, peering through her spectacles at the sky, listening intelligently. When Sasha finished she adjusted her eyeglasses and, looking directly at him, said in her harsh, mannish voice, "Do I understand that you wish me, through my brother, to find out about the prisoner—what is her name—Tamara? A poetic name, a very poetic name!

181

But I must tell you, my dear friend, that the task is not for me. Do you want to know why? I refuse to have anything to do with the security police."

"But your brother, the police sergeant—" Sasha tried to counter.

"My brother is the same as all the rest of them, the same security policeman. I won't have anything to do with him! I don't want to look at his face!"

This blow Sasha had not expected. But Sasha was not one of those people who lost courage at the first rebuff. He drew upon all his forces. He sent his father to the old lady, and the elder Safranovitch succeeded in convincing her to make peace with her brother, the security police sergeant, for their purpose. Within a few days Nadezhda Alexandrovna brought to the pharmacist an untidy bundle of information, confused, contradictory, misleading, impossible to decipher: something about a girl who had hanged herself in prison and an acquaintance of a man who had been sent off to his death.

"May they all go to the devil! May they all burn in hell! Leave me alone and don't ask me to dirty my hands any more! And listen to me, young man, spit in their faces, come to my garden today and I'll serve you some Yellow Spanish cherries that I myself grew—you never ate such cherries in your life! If I had more such trees I would be able to double if not triple the income from this garden."

Understandably, Sasha conveyed this information to Tamara's father in a delicate manner or, as his father the pharmacist would put it, "in a bitter pill coated in gold." Indeed, he coated the news in as much gold as he possibly could, and when Itzikl Shostepol, half in dread and half in hope, heard this prettied-up story, his face beamed, his eyes shone like those of a small child who had just been punished but then forgiven and presented with a toy!

"Now I know, now I understand—it's all because of that Romanenko, may his name and remembrance be erased. . . ."

From that day on Sasha did not rest. He broke through iron walls, as he himself expressed it, struck up acquaintances with people whom he would gladly have lived his entire life without ever knowing. He ferreted out secrets. With the help of money (Shostepol spared no expense) he succeeded in obtaining a copy of a letter from Tamara to a Party member with the name Marchenko. It was a passionate letter, full of fire. Sasha would have considered himself lucky if Tamara had written him, Sasha, such letters. . . . But he had to swallow it all. His own feelings toward Tamara didn't matter. It was necessary only to wrest her from the iron claws, to pull her from the abyss in which she was sinking deeper and deeper. Two matters were becoming interwoven: the name Marchenko was tied up with Romanenko, and Romanenko-Marchenko were linked to the story of Masha Bashevitch, who had so tragically put an end to her life.

Itzikl Shostepol became a frequent visitor in the pharmacist's home. He became friendly not only with the pharmacist's son but with the pharmacist himself and with Sasha Safranovitch's friend Kessler. It was quite a sight every evening to see a small conference of congenial people in the pharmacist's home: Solomon Safranovitch, Itzikl Shostepol, Sasha Safranovitch, and his friend Shimon Kessler. And they talked of only one person—Tamara—and of only one thing—how to free her.

"Do you know what I will tell you?" said Itzikl Shostepol to his wife, Shivka. "That Safranovitch [no longer "that pharmacist"] is quite a fine person. I like the way he deals with his son [no longer "that boy"] and the way he loves him and respects him—and there's good reason for it!"

The pharmacist too had changed his opinion of his neighbor Shostepol. He said to his son, "A pity on our Shostepol! [No longer "that Yiddash!"] I tell you, he isn't as crazy as I thought!"

7

All Is Calm

With giant strides the revolutionary movement was gathering momentum in the cities and towns, its great rallying cry resounding in one word—*Freedom*. As if at the command of a master mechanic or at the wave of a magic wand, the many wheels of the enormous machinery of daily life ground to a halt. It all stopped dead, and an eerie calm, an uncanny stillness, settled on the land. It was a kind of natural holiday, not a traditional holiday but the sort of holiday that people themselves create spontaneously. After many years of toil and strife, all at once people united under one standard and gathered in one place, announcing to one another, "Today let it be *Shabbos vayinefesh*—a true Sabbath of rest and revival!"

"Good yomtov to you!" said Yudel Katanti, stumbling into Nehemiah the shoemaker's, as tipsy as a Jew should be only on Simchas Torah. Perhaps it was because Yudel Katanti had already visited several fellow workers and had drunk a "L'chaim" in honor of the great holiday that "we workers" had created. Or perhaps it was because his *zogoisi*, as he called his wife in Hebrew, had chased him out of the house so he might find something for the Shabbos. Or perhaps his happiness derived from the fact that his "Kaddish," as he called his eldest son in Hebrew, had been transferred from one jail to another and it was likely he would be tried by court-martial or, as Yudel called it, *ba'chesed u'varachachamim*—tried with justice and compassion—meaning, with a rope around his neck and a hefty contribution to the state treasury.

"Serves him right. If a dog doesn't want to listen to the Megillah, he can't expect to eat hamantaschen!" Yudel spouted in his customary elegant way and received a dressing down from Nehemiah the shoemaker's wife, Zissel.

"You ought to be ashamed of yourself in every limb of your body! How can a man like yourself, in these times, not be ashamed to talk that way, making fun of his own son who risked his life for you and for me and for all of us? You're lucky my children aren't at home now. My Chaim would give you something to remember! I would never have believed it!" Zissel fumed. "A man like you sits there making fun of his own son who is sacrificing his life for everybody."

"For *everybody*?" said Yudel. "Everybody, I take it, sent my son a letter, 'My dear Reb Velvel! Since I, like the world, am sinking fast, I must have freedom. Therefore I am requesting of you, together with Nehemiah the shoemaker's two sons and with Chava's eldest son and with other such crusaders for our people, if you would be so kind, without fail, to come to our aid. . . . Sha! *Boruch haba'a*—Welcome! Reb Lippa is here!"

It was Lippa Bashevitch.

If Yudel Katanti had not declared it was Lippa Bashevitch, surely no one would have recognized him, because the wood hauler was entirely changed. His broom beard had turned white as snow and had spread across his face. The face itself had become a strange waxen yellow color and was as wrinkled as the wrong side of an old parchment Megillah. Under his hat, which was usually pulled down over his eyes, his hair had receded markedly in two deep recesses. His heart had been shattered. His kaftan was threadbare, one sleeve almost completely torn loose. He carried a large staff in his hand, and his eyes burned like coals, staring straight ahead. As he journeyed restlessly from house to house, arousing the people, predicting a great calamity, a deluge, a storm that was coming upon the world, he spoke in a dirgelike drone without pause.

"Hearken, O ye nations!" Lippa began with the Biblical intonation as he entered the home of Nehemiah the shoemaker. "Heed, O ye peoples of the world, what my mouth will utter now. Waken from your slumbers, raise your eyes, look about you and see the darkening sky. Black clouds are gathering above, a mighty wind drives them with great speed and they cover the entire sky. Soon, soon, a storm will be breaking. Soon, soon, the thunderclouds will burst and a great storm will pelt down, not of water but of blood. Rivers will overflow, flooding the houses, driving the people into the streets, where they will run like madmen, screaming and howling, looking heavenward, crying to God for help as the blood reaches their throats. But He doesn't hear them, this God. He is a God of vengeance. He cannot forget your sins and your guilt, your deception, your cheating and swindling and lying and spilling of innocent blood. . . ."

"Soon you'll hear him break into a strange chant,"

remarked Yudel Katanti, and Lippa Bashevitch abruptly changed from his earlier singsong into the chant from Lamentations and delivered his sermon thus: "Gather ye all together before the bloody deluge comes upon the world. Repent ye, pray ye, and say, *'Annah adonai hoshea nah*—egeden, magaden, magdaden!!!!'"

"Reb Lippa! Perhaps you would like something to eat?" Nehemiah's wife asked him.

"Eat?" Lippa repeated, and resumed in his prophetic vein. "Your own flesh shall you eat, ye will eat one another alive, a mother will devour her own child and children will make a feast of their parents, a brother will sell his own sister, a bridegroom his bride. The word 'mercy' shall be erased from the world until God's wrath is poured out in a great drowning, a deluge of blood and of tears. These are the tears of widows and orphans, of elderly fathers and mothers, of sisters and brothers who allowed themselves to be tormented by the impure evildoers and who refused to call upon God, to praise His name and sing aloud to Him, 'Egeden, magaden, magdaden! Eegeden, magaden, maagdaaden! Eeeeegeden, magaden, magdaaadden!!'"

"May all my enemies and may all your enemies and may all our gentile enemies have such a fate, God in heaven!" said Zissel, wiping her eyes with her apron.

Lippa Bashevitch continued to chant his prophecies; "Do you not see how stones are falling from the heavens? Molten stones, pitch and sulfur, and feathers, feathers, feathers without end? Do you not hear the cries of violated women, of dismembered children, of old people with spikes in their skulls? Do you not see bellies split open, stuffed with live cats?"

"Enough, enough, Reb Lippa, go in peace now!" Zissel said to him, ushering him out the door. And one could still hear from the other side of the door Lippa's same chant, his sorrowful, keening "Egeden, magaden, magdaden!" . . .

8

Mazel Tov! Mazel Tov!

How did this all come to pass? Where did all these people on the streets come from? What were students doing running through the streets since early morning, openly handing out leaflets to everyone they encountered? Why were people embracing one another in the middle of the street? Why were they kissing? Why were they congratulating one another? And where were the police? Why didn't one see any soldiers, Cossacks, security police?

The streets were filling with more and more people by the minute. No trams, no droshkys were anywhere in sight. Huge crowds were surging forward, on the move. The sidewalks as well as the roadways themselves were packed with people, their faces beaming, dressed in holiday clothes, red ribbons pinned near their hearts. Red banners had been hung on the doors of the houses, red tablecloths waved from the balconies, red flowers were on the windowsills. Just then a young girl wearing a red silk kerchief stopped and in a moment she tore the red kerchief from her head, shredded it into many small strips, and distributed them among the students who had surrounded her and were grabbing the red strips from her hand. Everyone was festive, happy, yet purposeful. A great, awesomely great event was taking place.

Itzikl Shostepol was still asleep when someone knocked on his door.

"Who is it?" Shostepol called.

"It's me, Safranovitch."

"Sasha? What is it?"

"Mazel tov—*constitutzia!*"

"What?"

"We've been granted a constitution. Get up, there's lots of excitement outside!"

"Shivka, do you hear?"

"God in heaven, what's happened?"

"Constitutzia!"

"Pardon me, may you be well, but what does that mean?" said Shivka to Sasha, and Itzikl became irked at her and attempted to explain it to her.

"What is there to understand? *Constitutzia* means a constitution!" And Itzikl nodded toward Sasha as if to say, "Go explain something to an old woman!"

But Sasha Safranovitch had more patience and explained to Madam Shostepol what *constitutzia* meant and added that as they had been granted a constitution, they could soon hope for amnesty.

"Do you understand? In a few hours we'll have the pleasure of seeing Tamara free right here in this very house!"

Sasha said this with such conviction that the parents looked at each other, lost control of themselves, and burst into tears. Sasha hastily took leave of the Shoste-pols and ran into his father on the steps.

"Sasha? Where are you coming from?"

"From the Shostepols'."

"Have you told them the news?"

"Well, of course."

"What did I tell you?"

"What *did* you tell me?"

"Constitutzia!"

"Wait, Papa, it's not over yet."

"What are you talking about, Sasha, God help you! Here's the newspaper, read it!"

"I've read it, I've read it."

"Nu?"

"Nu-nu!"

No more words were necessary. The father under-stood what the son meant. He knew him well. The pharmacist was upset with Sasha's response. He looked at him through his blue-tinted spectacles and wanted to say something more to him when they were interrupted by the old spinster with her dog, Hector. She threw her arms around the pharmacist's neck, kissed him, and congratulated him on the granting of the constitution and said that now all people would be equal. She also wanted to kiss the pharmacist's son, but Kessler came along and drew him away, leaving Nadezhda Alex-androvna together with the pharmacist. She looked at him through her spectacles and said in her mannish voice, "Just look at what's doing out there!"

What they saw cannot adequately be described. A flood of people poured into the main avenues from the side streets, merging like the streets themselves—merg-ing, growing, and gathering momentum. Not human beings but the streets themselves seemed to be moving, entire avenues, thick with heads like fields of corn sway-ing in a light breeze.

From the balconies and rooftops red banners were fluttering over the heads. Windows were bedecked with red. Everyone seemed to flow together as one—men, women, and children, gentile and Jew. The atmosphere was calm, relaxed, festive, as if a holiday were being celebrated in a house of worship. Not a trace of a policeman was to be seen. Although it was an October day, the sun was at peace with the earth for the sake of this great holiday; it was radiant, glowing and warm, as it would be on the most beautiful summer day. And from the side streets fresh oceans of people roared into the main arteries, carrying banners, merging with the great flood of heads as, with the impetus of a storm, they welcomed the magnificent holiday, the first day of freedom in that great land. Anthems could be heard, slogans were shouted, but the word shouted most often was *"Constitutzia! Constitutzia!"*

It was as if not only the people but the houses, the roofs, the streets, the trees, the city, the stones were crying *"Constitutzia!"* It was as if the earth itself was shaking as it cried out *"Con-sti-tu-tzia!"*

One person in that deluge of people sprang up on an overturned barrel and thundered out in a deep bass voice, which one could recognize as belonging to the hairy Mischa Berezniak-Neiditch: "Citizens! This is the first time you are being addressed by that title of freedom, 'citizens'! Allow me, a stranger, to congratulate you on your magnificent holiday, on your great triumph! Citizens! We celebrate your victory, we delight in your holiday! But let us not forget our fallen comrades, those who shed their blood, those who sacrificed their lives, those who died on the scaffold for us and for our freedom. Fall to your knees, one and all!"

And the vast audience dropped to its knees as one person, and the speaker did the same on the overturned barrel, raising his hands and declaiming in his bass voice the mournful Russian song "*Vi zshertvoyu poli*—You offered up your lives . . ."

And the flood of human beings joined in the lament as one. The red flags were lowered, and all heads bowed as they sang—many, many weeping, because many, many had members of the family and friends among those who had fallen. A holy stillness descended upon the mass of uncovered heads of those who had assembled there in the name of freedom.

And when the speaker rose to his feet the flood of people rose with him, and his bass voice thundered on: "Citizens! We have honored our fallen fighters. Now we must remember those crusaders who have not fallen. They are alive and are suffering in the crowded, dark prisons. Remember them! They do not yet know of our great celebration, which they made possible for us. Let us go to them! Let us free the martyrs for our freedom! All of us, as one person, let us go to the prisons! Let no one stay behind. Let us demand amnesty for our sisters and brothers! Let them be freed immediately. Let them open the doors and release the innocent! And should they meet us with gunfire, then we are prepared to fall! To the prisons, citizens, to the prisons!"

The earth that bore that old city had never heard such a sound, a sound loud enough to topple walls. The sky that blanketed the earth had never witnessed such swarms of people. The sun forgot it was an October day and its beaming face joyfully looked down on the excited, happy throng. Nature itself was participating in that extraordinary, bright, blessed day of freedom.

9

The Holiday Spoiled

Wonder of wonders! How on earth were people in that
flood able to find one another? Only people with a special talent, such as the clever Sasha Safranovitch and his
friend Kessler, could manage it. The two friends, el-
bowing their way, forced a path for themselves through
the crowd toward the prisons, and on the way ran into
Itzikl Shostepol, who had been drawn from his house,
umbrella in hand, not knowing what power held sway
over him.

Shostepol couldn't have been happier to see his own
child than he was to see the pharmacist's son. Was it
really true? Was it all really happening? A constitution?
All were equal? Even Jews? They would free the political prisoners? And he would soon see his daughter free?
His beloved one and only dear daughter? He looked
around him, marveling at how those "boys," those
"good-for-nothings" had prevailed! He encountered

Jews he knew who congratulated him: "Today we are the equals of everyone!" No longer were they wondering, *Are* we the equals of everyone? Not just Jews, but friendly gentiles greeted him, kissed him, gave him a mazel tov. Had the Messiah come? He felt a hand on his shoulder and turned his head. "Sasha?"

Itzikl took Sasha's arm and looked directly into his eyes, as if to say, "Is this a dream?" And Sasha Safranovitch, as if realizing what he was thinking, said to him with a smile, "It's true. We're going to set them free. In just half an hour Tamara will be here with us . . . with us!"

"God be willing!" said Itzikl, his face expressing the fear that he might be hoping for too much, and he squeezed Sasha's hand. "Is it possible that this time we've gotten what we want?" The word "we" was said by Itzikl Shostepol with pride now, not so much referring to himself but to his daughter. . . . And he caught sight in the throng of people of a familiar-looking girl with a young man, walking arm in arm in a festive mood. He could have sworn it was Chaska and her fiancé.

It's a holiday, he thought. We are all equal. However pleased he might have felt that all were now equal, there was still a bit of resentment over it. How appropriate was it that his housemaid, Chaska, should be the equal of his daughter, Tamara? Then again, he thought, to the devil with it, *let* them be equal. Just let him live to see his daughter in good health! He recognized another familiar face in the crush of people—Netchiporenko, the police commissioner's clerk. What's that goy doing here? he thought, unable to restrain himself from winking at him and flourishing his umbrella, his head held high with pride.

"Where is Anton Ivanovitch? How come we don't see him at our festivities?"

Netchiporenko lowered his eyes and shook his head without answering Shostepol. One didn't know whether he was pleased or not.

"That's the police commissioner's right-hand man," said Shostepol to Sasha, crowing. But Sasha was absorbed in something he saw elsewhere. He saw his father walking arm in arm with his neighbor Nadezhda Alexandrova, both looking as cheerful as newlyweds. On every face was written great joy in this great holiday!

A tumultuous "Hoorah!"—a new wave of people. An indescribable enthusiasm gripped the huge mass. The doors of the prisons had been flung open by the governor himself, who was making a speech on the release of the prisoners, each of whom the crowd greeted with the wildest excitement. There seemed to be no limit to the rapture of the multitude as waves of delirious joy swept through the horde.

"Long live freedom! Long live the prisoners!"

Everyone pressed forward to look at the freed prisoners. Some wanted to see them only because of curiousity, others because of personal interest—to catch sight of a relative, a child, a good friend. And in order to make the celebration more nearly complete, and so that the entire city would know of the amnesty, the liberated prisoners were paraded to the accompaniment of music, with song and with shouts of "Hoorah!" through the main streets of the city. Every so often a platform would be improvised and one of the released prisoners presented and asked to say a word, just a few words— and "hoorahs" would drown out his voice.

Suddenly the crowd became unruly. People began pushing and shoving. And on the makeshift platform there appeared a very pretty girl with black curly hair, with a Jewish nose and lovely large dark eyes. Itzikl Shostepol, who until then had been holding onto the arm of his young friend Sasha Safranovitch, threw himself forward and, stretching his arms out, cried, "My daughter! My clever, dear dau—"

The ecstatic father could say no more. He was cut off in mid-word. A strange thing happened that no one could have foreseen, which no one could have imagined while either awake or dreaming, which spoiled this most joyful holiday—destroyed, wrecked it for a long, long time, if not forever. Suddenly and unexpectedly the sound of gunfire was heard—no one could tell from which direction—and the sea of heads gradually, gradually began to sway, and everything took on an eerie appearance.

As from a sweet slumber or from a pleasant dream, the multitude was jolted awake, and an icy dread gripped them. Suddenly a panic, a stampede, swept through the stunned crowd. People began running and leaping over one another, an earthquake. Totally ignorant of what was happening, each individual instinctively thought only of himself, of how to come out of there alive. And each one attempted to save only himself. Sasha Safranovitch's first thought was of Tamara— where was Tamara? How could he reach her and pull her from this mob? Instead of running to escape as everyone around him was doing, he pushed his way in the opposite direction, leaping over the fallen, to where Tamara had just been standing. He began to work his way through the crowd with the force of his bare elbows, unmindful of every danger, until he finally reached the edge of the crowd, the very place where the speaker's platform was located. When he saw the confused Tamara among the many bewildered people he grasped her by the arm, yanked her out of the mass of humanity, and, with the same force of his bony elbows, made his way over the dead and over the living, succeeding in extricating them both from the crush and finally reaching a small space free of people.

At first Tamara couldn't figure out what she was doing or where she was going or with whom. Afterward, when she had emerged from the mob of people into the open space, she looked back and saw blood, the blood of those who had been shot, killed, trampled. She tore herself away from Sasha's grip and wanted to run back. But Sasha Safranovitch was determined not to let her go, and he held her back with his thin but powerful hands. "You are not going back there!"

Unnecessary words. It was impossible to go back in any case. One could go only forward—and not simply go, but run, because a solid wave of people, like an incoming tide, was carrying them, carrying them . . .

And from the rear, shooting was heard . . . and horses were trampling people . . .

Not until they had reached No. 13 Vasilchikover Street, at Solomon Safranovitch's pharmacy, did Tamara notice that her savior was holding his left hand to his right shoulder and that his face was as ashen as that of a corpse.

"What's the matter?" she asked him, embarrassed to look directly into his eyes.

"Nothing, nothing, nothing to worry about." Sasha answered her with an amiable little smile, pointing to his shoulder and lowering himself carefully to the ground. Tamara bent over him and lifted him with both hands as one would a child, and, with all her strength, she made her way to the door and rang the bell repeatedly until Chava, the old woman, Chaska, the kitchenmaid, and the gentile janitor ran out, and they carried the wounded Sasha to Itzikl Shostepol's apartment (the pharmacist's apartment was locked). And not till he had been placed on a sofa and his shirt unbuttoned did they see he was covered with blood. Sasha fainted.

"A doctor! Water! Ice! The pharmacist!" And they all sprang into action, this one for water, that one for ice, another for the doctor. Shivka, once she knew that Tamara had been freed (Nehemiah the shoemaker's wife had earned the mitzvah by rushing home to tell the news before anyone else), ran into the street shouting and met her husband, who was running home more dead than alive.

When he saw Shivka running toward him, Itzikl Shostepol became terror-stricken. With his umbrella he signaled her from a distance to go back because it was dangerous.

"They're shooting!" he shouted to her.

"They're shooting?"

"They're shooting! They're shooting! Go back!"

"Here too," Shivka answered him. "They've already shot someone!"

"Where? Who?" Itzikl screamed, almost fainting.

"They've shot the pharmacist's son."

The bullet was removed from the wounded Safranovitch and he was bandaged. The doctor said that he was not in danger; the patient would be on his feet in three or four days. He cautioned them to check his temperature regularly; otherwise there was nothing to worry about. The patient talked, joked, and felt quite well. And how could he *not* feel well when Tamara was sitting beside him along with the others? She herself had insisted on sitting with the patient. Itzikl Shostepol had wanted her to rest after her ordeal, and in addition her mother hadn't seen her in such a long time. But Tamara said she would not budge from the patient's side.

As she sat there Tamara had a chance to think over for

the first time since she had known Safranovitch all that had happened between them until that moment. It was the first time, one could say, that Tamara had allowed herself to become so close to this person. And she was reminded of how this Safranovitch had followed her around from childhood on, like a shadow. . . . And later, when he was a little older, a teenager, he was forever underfoot, always blushing and bashful. . . . And then when he went to Petersburg with her and was afraid to approach her . . . Then in Petersburg their meetings and discussions. "They made me the keeper of the vineyards, but mine own vineyard have I not kept . . ."

Tamara pondered on the meaning of that verse and all she had really contributed to the movement. She was no more than a passive, marginal person. What had she herself achieved? Nothing at all! In what way had she had any greater part in the constitution than, say, her mother? A whole procession of activists passed through her mind: Romanenko, Masha, Berezniak, and many others. What was she to them but a good friend and nothing more? Why did all the others have some contribution to make and she none? Twice she had sat in prison, and each time on the sidelines, a hanger-on and never as active a participant as the others. She wanted so much to be active! Here was Safranovitch, who wasn't a revolutionary and yet always had so much to do as a nationalist for his own people. Were not *his* people *her* people? Was she not more responsible, as Sasha said, for her own people than for others, for whom she was wearing herself out and breaking her heart and for whom she was prepared to sacrifice her life?

"How is he?" Shostepol asked, tiptoeing over to the bed where Sasha was lying and where his daughter and Sasha's friend Kessler were sitting on either side of him.

"He's asleep," Tamara said quietly.

"Shhh . . . he's asleep!" said Itzikl Shostepol to Shivka, who was coming up behind him.

At that moment Chava, the old woman, burst in with news for her employer, Itzikl Shostepol. "Sir, they say something lively is happening on the Jewish Street!"

"Shhh . . . What do you mean, 'lively'?" Itzikl asked.

"A pogrom, they say,"

They all sprang from their seats.

"A what?"

"Don't you know what a pogrom is? A Jewish pogrom, the same as in Kishinev," responded Chava.

That quintessentially Russian word "pogrom," which cannot be translated into any other language in the world, evokes in Jews an emotion that no other people can comprehend. As bizarre as it may sound, at that moment, on that very day, it sounded even more bizarre than ever. A pogrom on *that* day? How was it possible?

No sooner had Chava delivered her news than Nehemiah the shoemaker entered with his two sons, fear written on their faces.

"They're attacking people!" said Chaim, and Benny echoed, "They're attacking people—it's a pogrom."

They were all riveted to the spot. Sasha sat up, propped himself up on his elbow; his eyes and Tamara's eyes met. In that look everything was expressed that until that moment had remained unspoken.

Nehemiah felt it necessary to calm his neighbors. "Don't be afraid—it might be worse. They're attacking only poor people. On the Jewish Street it's an organized pogrom. I just had a visit from a friend of mine, a tailor, Yudel Katanti—"

"Enough with your tailor Katanti!" Itzikl Shostepol let his anger out on the shoemaker, as if the shoemaker were responsible for what was going on.

Tamara stood up, her face flushed, her eyes flashing. "It's a lie! It can't be! It can't be!"

"Why can't it be? It certainly *can* be!" said Sasha, agitated. "This is the true epilogue, which should have been foreseen—"

"You must lie still!" Tamara interrupted him in a gentle tone that Sasha had never heard from her. "The doctor told you to lie quietly. . . . I'm going now but will be right back. . . . Lie quietly!"

Sasha obeyed like a child and lay down, appearing to be calm, and watched as Tamara put on her coat, preparing to leave. How could he remain alone, without her? He felt as if he had to get up from the sofa. He felt as if something was compelling him to spring up, to throw himself at her feet and cry, "No, you won't go alone, Tamara, you'll go with me! With me! With me!"

Tamara left, and Sasha remained lying in a burning fever. His temperature had risen.

10

What Tamara Saw and Heard

It was still early when Tamara started out for the poor section of town, the Jewish Street. On the way she encountered women with children, laden with bundles of old clothing, riding on carts, one cart after another. Their frightened faces expressed shame, as if they were the ones who were committing a crime. . . . Where were they going? They themselves didn't know. They had heard there was a pogrom and they had to seek refuge—one with a friendly gentile, another in a hotel, and others at the train station. But they couldn't get very far, because they weren't permitted to: they were being stopped and the horses turned back. Tamara went over to a policeman and asked him how he could allow such a thing to happen. She was told that the "Barishni" had better get out of there in a hurry or she might very well share the same fate as those Jews.

"Why just Jews?" Tamara asked him.

"Because that's the kind of day it is," the policeman answered her, in a tone of voice that conveyed that shedding blood in the streets was an ordinary, everyday event.

Tamara went farther and came on a poor Jewish woman, still young, with two children—one in her arms, the other holding her hand—who was running, clutching a basket and being chased by two gentile women. One was grabbing for the basket and the other was tearing the shawl from the young women's head. Tamara ran over and stopped them. "God be with you—why are you doing that?"

"Today we can!" The gentile women answered her with a laugh and let go of the poor woman. Tamara found out from her that she was fleeing from the Jewish Street, where they were massacring Jews. She had no idea where she was running to, but she had reasoned that among the more well-to-do, and especially among the gentiles, they probably wouldn't attack her, and perhaps someone might even take pity on her and her two orphans. She would prefer to take refuge in a friendly gentile home, which would be safer.

Tamara thought it would be a good idea to hide this woman with a gentile. But who? It wasn't far from the Gymnasium—with Frau Romanenko! She told the young woman she would take her to a gentile acquaintance of hers. "To a gentile? God bless you!" The young woman tried to embrace and kiss her. Tamara grabbed her by the hand and ran with her, and while they were running the woman told Tamara of a thousand atrocities that had taken place on the Jewish Street. They were beating, murdering, slaughtering. Tamara didn't want to hear any of this and involuntarily was reminded of Bialik's bloody poem that Sasha had once read to her and that had at the time impressed her as beautiful, lofty poetry and nothing more. Now the verses rang in her ears like trumpets, like a thousand kettledrums:

> Where are their fists? Where is their thunder
> That should settle the score
> For all the generations . . .

She was tempted to go back to take up whatever weapon might come to hand, to be avenged, to settle the score for all that spilled blood. But she remembered she had taken it upon herself to deliver this young woman and her children to a gentile. They had reached the Gymnasium where her gentile acquaintance lived.

"Here you'll be safe!" Tamara said to the young woman as she rang the doorbell once, twice, and a third time. There was no answer. She then rang at the main gate, and a servant appeared. Seeing they were Jews, he became infuriated. "This is no Jewish synagogue! Get out of here before they break every bone in your body!"

"You'd better go," said the young woman to Tamara. "I'm staying here, no matter what happens. Even among gentiles, someone will take pity on me. I'm a poor widow with two tiny orphans. What can they take from me?"

Tamara left them and saw in the distance a procession of people carrying the national flag. What could it mean? She saw from afar now—they were breaking down doors, shattering windows, throwing, flinging, whipping, and hurling. Young gentile boys and girls were beating people, and she saw how many were falling and were being trampled by horses. . . . Tamara saw that the procession had suddenly halted near the

Gymnasium. . . . On the balcony stood old Romanenko, bareheaded, nodding this way and that, and a
frightful "Hoorah!" was heard.

"Down with the constitution! Death to the Jews!"

"Hoorah! Death to the Jews!"

11

The Storm Spreads

The pharmacist Solomon Safranovitch was a lucky sur-
vivor. After the first shot he was swept away from his
friend Nadezhda Alexandrovna and carried along with
the current of people to the other side of the city, into
the distant avenues and side streets where he hadn't been
for years. He heard strange cries from afar and he
thought these might be the cries of people screaming
and calling for help. His heart sank and he wanted to
turn back. Without knowing where he was going, he
decided to walk downhill to the Jewish Street. There he
encountered the sort of strange-looking creatures he had
not seen for so long: barefoot, bedraggled, with swollen
faces, red noses, bruised eyes. Each one was carrying an
armful of household goods and was rushing with the
urgency of one preparing for a holiday or one who is
making a hurried delivery and must return for another
trip or else it would be too late. . . . Among the objects

these people were carrying were new boots and old galoshes, new blankets and old sacks, silver vases, papier-mâché poodles, iron pots, packages of tea, porcelain clocks, loaves of sugar, and other such incongruous collections.

Not fully realizing what was going on but sensing that it was not good, he became anxious to return home. But a strange power drew him ever farther and farther until on another street he was confronted by a gang of young gentile boys brandishing cudgels. They stopped him and asked how much money he was carrying. Naturally the pharmacist stood up to them defiantly. What right did they have to stop a peaceful citizen in the middle of the street, and especially at such a time when the constitution had been given?"

"Constitution, is it?" the young thugs replied to the pharmacist, and honored him with a blessing on his head so soundly that he was staggered, lost his hat and his blue-tinted spectacles, and fell to the ground. The hoodlums removed his gold watch and chain and shook out all his pockets, after which they got into an argument about whether he was a Jew or a Christian. If he was a Christian, how come he was a redhead? If he was a Jew, why was he clean-shaven? And they all agreed they would ask him himself. Needless to say, the pharmacist immediately said he was a Christian, a true Christian.

"If he's a Christian, let him prove it. Let him cross himself three times!" demanded the boys, and the poor pharmacist, terrified for his life, had to cross himself three times.

"A Jew can cross himself too!" one of the smarter ones decided. "Let him show us that he's wearing a crucifix."

Here he realized he was in trouble. Who could tell

what this gang of ruffians might do to him? An idea came to him. Not for nothing do Jews have a reputation for being resourceful. And he pretended to confess to them that his ancestors were Jewish and he himself was once a Jew, but now he was a Christian.

So where was his crucifix?

"I'm a Protestant!" the pharmacist explained on the spur of the moment, and begged them to have mercy on him. He had a sick wife and four small children and an elderly mother and a blind father. (In the cause of survival, and since he had already started making up a story, he embroidered it further.)

And the young thugs took pity on the converted Protestant who had a sick wife and four small children and an elderly mother and a blind father and took from him only his clothes and shoes, leaving him in his shirt and stockings, and for good measure granted him a few blows because he was Protestant and not Greek Orthodox.

"If you were already converting, you should have taken on the true Greek Orthodox faith, not end up a Protestant. The next time you convert, do it the right way."

The miraculously spared pharmacist Safranovitch gave thanks to God for having narrowly escaped a death with which he had just come face-to-face. He was not aware that back home not a scrap remained of his pharmacy and of his worldly goods. Luckily his neighbor Nadezhda Alexandrovna had at least been able to save his apartment and his son, Sasha. Had she arrived half an hour earlier, perhaps she could have saved the pharmacy as well. As soon as the good Nadezhda Alexandrovna came home and realized what was happening, that the city was in turmoil, she went straight to her friend Safranovitch to see what was going on there, and arrived just in time to observe the mob falling to its work. Seeing the wreckage left of the pharmacy, she became frightened. She discovered a band of hooligans at the back door ready to break into the house and continue their work. She screamed loudly at them to leave immediately or else she would call out a company of Cossacks! She was a state prosecutor's sister and wouldn't allow them to touch this house. It was *her* house! "This is terrible! An outrage!"

"We don't want your house, we just want the Jews who live here!" the hoodlums answered her.

"There are no Jews here! Get out of here! This is terrible! An outrage!"

And Nadezhda Alexandrovna was fierce in her unbridled rage. The ruffians took stock of the situation—there were plenty of Jews in the city, time was moving on. And so they stepped back and went off to another house.

Itzikl Shostepol and his wife, Shivka, who were standing at the window in a state of absolute terror, not knowing which way to turn, saw that the vandals had suddenly turned away from their door, and they thanked God that they had miraculously been spared from a great danger, but they were unaware of exactly who had been responsible for this miracle.

Sasha's friend Kessler was also standing at the window, reporting to Sasha on the activities outside. Sasha had promised Tamara he wouldn't budge from his bed. No matter what might happen, he was going to keep his word unless the pogrom'chiks were to break into the house! Kessler had even barricaded the door with chests of drawers and chairs. A loaded revolver was also at hand. He was prepared to shoot anyone who might show his face at the door. He would allow no one to approach his wounded friend. They would have to kill him first!

"That band of hoodlums has turned away from our house and is going somewhere else," Kessler reported to his friend the wounded Sasha. Itzikl Shostepol, glued to the window, saw the police commissioner, Anton Ivanovitch Kholodkov, riding by on his horse with the graceful posting motion of an officer, indicating something with his hand but not chasing off the bullies. Itzikl Shostepol opened the window and wanted to shout to Anton Ivanovitch to come to their aid and to chase off those drunkards, but Shivka wouldn't let him. She held him fast by the hand.

"Itzi! Don't open the window! They'll kill us, Itzi!"

Itzikl Shostepol slammed the window shut, but through the panes could be heard eerie echoes of strange cries, thousands of cries, an odd mixture of screaming and weeping, of people pleading to be spared and of people who were shouting, "Down with the Yids!" He could hear a command given, then a volley of rifle fire, the sound of shattering glass, and a frightful "Hoorah!" drowning out the screams.

Was the world coming to an end?

But Nehemiah the shoemaker's children, Yudel Katanti's eldest son, Chava's "Disaster," Berezniak-Neiditch, and other comrades did not wait for an invitation. As soon as they heard it was "lively" on the Jewish Street they immediately called their friends together to get ready. After they distributed weapons they dispersed, and many of them proceeded to the Jewish Street. Wherever there was trouble they interceded. With their revolvers they drove the hoodlums away like crows. So it went from one street to the next; but then on one street their luck ran out. They encountered strong resistance and began to fall, one at a time, like so many straws.

Among the first victims was Nehemiah the shoemaker's younger son, Benny, who was slain by two bullets that punctured his lungs and heart.

Two comrades lifted him in their arms, like a felled deer in the hunt, and quickly brought him home, where only his mother was to be found. His brother, Chaim, was with his comrades at another place, and his father, Nehemiah, had gone with his friend Yudel Katanti to find out what was happening.

As was to be expected, Yudel Katanti was in his usual high spirits, especially because that very morning, in honor of the great holiday, he had downed quite a few, and so was spouting his Biblical verses and laughing at the constitution, holding his sides with laughter. Teasing the shoemaker, boasting that he knew beforehand, may he have a good life in this world and in the next world, that it would all have to end up this way, ha-ha-ha!

But the cheerful tailor wasn't allowed to laugh for long. When they heard that the pogrom had reached Vasilchikover Street the two of them started for home, and when they arrived they found the street already besieged. They barely made it to Safronovitch's pharmacy.

"Yudel, we're in trouble!" said Nehemiah.

As he spoke those words the distraught deranged Lippa Bashevitch came by, hatless, his hair disheveled, a staff in his hand, preaching still in the manner of Isaiah: "And there will come a plague upon your bodies and you will seek help and you shall cry out and no one will answer you, for great is the fury of God who sits in judgment over the world with his great windstorm which he has sent upon the earth because you refused to

obey his commandment—egeden, magaden, magdaden! Eegeeden, magaden, magdaaaden! Eeegeeden,
magaden, magdaaaaden! . . ."

Tragic, most tragic was that day's end, a day that had
begun in such joy and happiness. Silently the dark night
descended on the earth and spread its black wings over
the melancholy world. After that too joyous and happy
day the night appeared like a window dressed in mourning weeks. Silence reigned. No passerby, no traveler.
The theaters were closed, the restaurants bolted shut,
the streetlamps extinguished. All was gloomy, silent.
Occasionally from a distance one could hear the echo of
a hoarse "Hoorah!," the wailing of someone being
beaten, cries for help, the song of a drunkard—sounds
that rose up and then died down. And again it was still.
Silently the brooding sky peered down with its billions
of twinkling worlds upon the small dark earth, whose
inhabitants were convinced that because of them God
had created this vast, multitudinous, billion-planeted
universe. Silent. Dark. Gloomy.

This silent, dark, gloomy night refused to reveal what
had taken place in the gloomy, poor, filthy Jewish
houses and shacks, refused to reveal what had happened
to the humiliated, poor, hungry, miserable, naked,
barefoot, castaway, forgotten, and dejected Jews. . . .
No, it would not tell, that silent, gloomy night, what
had taken place there! The night also refused to reveal
the silent, dark, furtive meetings taking place in the
silent, dark, secret cellars where silent, dark, furtive
people were distributing assignments in order to prepare for the day after. And many, many more things
were accomplished in that silent, dark, gloomy night. It
would come, that hoped-for, bright morning. It would
come, and everything would be told when the troubles
were over.

12

Eternal Wanderers

It was a wet, cold morning, one of those wet, cold autumn days of which it is said, "It's a pity to let a dog out on a day like this." The train station where Shostepol had once met Safranovitch the pharmacist when their children were arriving from Petersburg for Pesach was now densely packed with people, mainly in the third-class waiting room. It was hardly possible to breathe. Most of those waiting were Jews. One could say they were all Jews. All crowded together, sitting or standing, were women and children with valises, sacks, packages, and pillows, pillows, pillows! Their faces were terrified, their eyes darting about in every direction. They trembled when they heard a shout or even a whistle. . . . From the way they were talking one could surmise that these were emigrants, because one could hear the words, "escort," "Hamburg," "ship ticket," "America." The word "America" was heard more often than any other. The word "America" had for them a special magnetism, a kind of magical meaning. It stood for an ideal of which many, many had long dreamed. They imagined America to be a kind of heaven, a sort of Paradise. "We hope, God Almighty, they will let us in and not, God forbid, send us back."

The shouting was deafening. The uproar and the running and shoving and pushing were overwhelming. Among the multitude could be seen many with bandaged heads, bruised eyes, evidence of the not-yet-healed, not-yet-subsided pogrom. . . .

"Do you think they'll let you into America looking like that?" an impudent boy, his hands thrust into his pockets, teased an old woman, her face yellow with jaundice and her brow knit with worry.

"May your mother have boils!" the old woman cursed him. "As long as my eyes remain healthy I'm all right. You can go to hell!"

A young mother with a nursing baby tugged at an old man's coat. She wanted to know if they permitted mothers with nursing babies into America. The old man was rocking back and forth as he recited his prayers and couldn't answer her, but instead he gesticulated, indicating You're a poor, stupid cow!—meanwhile looking around him to make sure no policeman saw him praying.

A family was sitting off in a corner. They had four boys and two girls. Boys, they said, in America, were a blessing, they can go to work. Girls, they said, were also a blessing, they can go to work. There was also a grandmother and a grandfather. The grandmother would have gone to America with the children, but she couldn't, because the grandfather was blind. They didn't allow blind people into America. She would have to remain with the old man. Unless, perhaps, one day, if a miracle were to take place and they would send her a ship ticket from over there . . . Meanwhile let him live out his years. It was enough that God had punished him and both his eyes had been poked out during the pogrom because he refused to divulge where the children's money was hidden—twenty-two rubles. . . . The old grandfather stroked his grandchildren's heads, tears streaming from his blinded eyes, and said to them, "It seems that I'll never ever see you again, children! Never ever see you anymore!"

Among the emigrants one could spot Nehemiah the shoemaker, his wife, Zissel, and their elder son, Chaim. The younger one, Benny, was lying in hallowed ground but without a gravestone. They had sold all their possessions and were going to a land from which they would probably never return.

"You're wrong, old man, we'll all come back, and *I* certainly will." So Chaim said to his father as he tried to convince him that he, Chaim, wasn't going to America for good; and he wasn't going there for his own sake but for theirs. Should things blow over here, they would all come back "home," as they were all now going to America.

"God willing!" broke in an utter stranger, who was cutting thin slices of bread with a small sharp knife and spreading the bread with egg yolk. He borrowed a small handful of salt from another stranger, a woman with a tear-streaked face.

"Going here, going there, Yisraelik is always on the move!" exclaimed the old Jew who had been praying and was now folding up the tallis and putting away the tefillin, his cheeks flushed. "Our people of Israel, you understand, are fulfilling the commandment that God once gave to our Father Abraham: *"Lech-l'cha"*—Get thee out from thy land and from thy birthplace and from they father's house . . .

"A lot of good it's done us!" cried out another bystander, with a growth on his eyelid, and a third one, also a complete stranger, just a young man and a bit of an intellectual by appearance, without peyes and with a closely trimmed beard in the modern manner, added, "It *has* done us a lot of good, because wandering in the Diaspora—that's our commandment, our mission. Do you understand that or not? On the day that the Jews stop wandering in the Diaspora they will, God forbid, on that day stop being Jews."

Noting that the crowd was staring at him in astonishment, he explained himself. "You think that's *my* idea? That's what a great, truly great man has said." And he continued his discourse in a singsong, accentuating his points with an artful turning out of his thumb. "Especially now," he said, "when we are in disgrace, it is required of us that we be *more* honest and *more* righteous and better and finer than all the others. But what expectations can other nations have of us," he said, "when we will be as other nations in our own land? No, brothers! Our mission is to wander, always to dwell among strangers, to be a witness, to set an example for all. Do you understand that or not?"

The circle around the young man had grown larger and wider by the minute. Jews love to hear a good speech, no matter where or when, even in the minutes before catching a train. The men, who understood, assumed the young man had to be a Zionist, because he spoke too well and too passionately. And the women, who didn't understand at all, nodded along, sighing, and were prepared to shed a tear at any moment, as if a rabbi were speaking.

Amid the crowd that encircled the young intellectual

was Sasha Safranovitch, who had come to see his father off. The pharmacist was going to Palestine to be a pharmacist there. If it would be necessary for him to take an examination, he would take it. Such an unforeseen metamorphosis could have been accomplished only by the storm through which he had lived and all its consequences. In fact, Solomon Safranovitch had originally planned to go to America, but it was his son who had insisted he emigrate to Palestine. There were no two ways about it—after all, he was a one and only son. Sasha would remain until he graduated, when he too would emigrate to Palestine. Palestine and America— what a choice! Most touching of all was the fact that the pharmacist's Christian friend Nadezhda Alexandrovna had convinced her friend the pharmacist that it was better for him to go to Palestine. "Palestine," she had said, with awe in her voice, "Palestine is your homeland, your fatherland. How can you forsake it for a strange land, for America? It's terrible! An outrage!"

Contributing in large part to this decision was also Itzikl Shostepol, who was now more than a neighbor and most likely a future in-law. It was not, as yet, official, understand, it was still a secret, but the kind of secret that everyone knew and about which everyone was talking and whispering. Any day now it might become a fact. In the meanwhile the children had to finish their studies. They would both be going back soon to Petersburg. Of late they had been so close to each other that no one had any doubt at all that they would marry. There was but one small obstacle: the bridegroom was a Zionist, and a dedicated Zionist at that, while the bride was as yet cold toward Zionism, quite cold. But *Mah she'lo ya'aseh ha'seychl ya'aseh haz'man*—What reason will not do, time will accomplish. Itzikl Shostepol quoted a verse to his semiofficial in-law, the pharmacist, who, although he knew no Hebrew, nevertheless peered over his spectacles approvingly.

"Alexander Solomonovitch, where did you go? It's terrible! An outrage!" Nadezhda Alexandrovna cried out and clapped her hands together when she saw Sasha Safranovitch in the third-class crowd surrounding the young intellectual. Following closely on her heels were the pharmacist, who during this trying time had turned quite pale, Tamara, and Itzikl Shostepol, who himself had aged considerably. His eyes had become puffy with little bags beneath them. His daughter, Tamara, had also changed—she had become even more beautiful than before.

"What's happening here?" Tamara asked.

"Our wanderers," Sasha answered her, indicating the crowd of emigrants with his eyes, "our eternal wanderers."

"The eternal wanderers!" Nadezhda Alexandrovna echoed in a mannish, melancholy tone of voice, but she soon threw her arms around her good friend. "Why are we standing here? It's time to say goodbye!" And she exclaimed her usual, "It's terrible! An outrage!"

And the little group, which had grown so close, walked out on the station platform, and there they bade farewell to the pharmacist Safranovitch, and they kissed him and wished him well with all their hearts.

PLUME Quality Paperbacks For Your Enjoyment

☐ **THE PRIME OF MISS JEAN BRODIE. Muriel Spark.** A dazzling psychological study, a darkly fascinating tale of treachery and passion, this remarkable work of fiction, set in the 1930's probes the human heart with humor, style and the penetrating bite of truth.

(255899—$6.95)*

☐ **FABLES AND FAIRY TALES. Leo Tolstoy.** Splendidly translated by Ann Dunnigan, whose recent version of War and Peace has been acclaimed the finest of modern English renderings, these fables and fairy tales offer a supreme example of a great writer in whom artist and moralist become one. (254876—$5.95)

☐ **THE FOUR-GATED CITY. Doris Lessing.** Themes of time, sex, politics, society, and self are interwoven in a vivid portrayal of individual fate against the backdrop of modern civilization. (256968—$9.95)

☐ **THE ICE AGE. Margaret Drabble.** The best-known and most ambitious of Margaret Drabble's novels explores the lives and loves of a group of people each of whom is at a turning point in his or her life.

(256801—$6.95)*

All prices higher in Canada.

*Not available in Canada.

To order please use coupon on the next page.

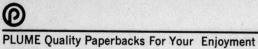

PLUME Quality Paperbacks For Your Enjoyment

(0452)

☐ **FLIGHTS. Jim Shepard.** Warmhearted and funny, Flights tells an achingly truthful story of family happiness and family pain, with soaring escape from childhood at its triumphant climax.   (255929—$6.95)

☐ **THE GARRICK YEAR. Margaret Drabble.** A sly, sharp comedy of erotic errors. The Garrick Year glosses the difference between modern love and modern marriage with wit and sophistication. (255902—$6.95)

☐ **THE FAMILY OF MAX DESIR.** A young man painfully divided between his family and his lover.   (255872—$6.95)

☐ **MANTISSA. John Fowles.** A teasingly enigmatic dialogue of words and flesh. A slyly dazzling exposition of connections made and missed, of postures assumed and abandoned. A virtuoso performance by a great contemporary storyteller.   (254299—$6.95)

All prices higher in Canada.

*Not available in Canada.

To order please use coupon on the next page.